SEVEN

Sons

LILI SAINT GERMAIN

Formatting by Inkstain Interior Book Designing
Produced by Lili Saint Germain at Lili Saint Germain Publishing

www.lilistgermain.blogspot.com

For everyone who has ever dreamed of revenge

Confucius said, "Before embarking upon a journey of revenge, dig two graves."

I planned to dig seven.

ONE

SOMETIMES I DON'T THINK ABOUT it for hours at a time. Sometimes, a whole day will pass, and it'll be there, under the surface, burning my insides with the brutality of its truth. *My truth.*

And I'll get home from my dead-end job in this dead-end fucking town in the asshole of Nebraska, and I'll have almost made it through a whole day of not thinking about it, about my father and Dornan Ross and his sons.

But then I'll do something without thinking, like undress to go to bed, or slide under the covers of my bed. And I'll see the marks they branded on my right hip – seven horizontal lines, each stacked on top of each other, made by casting the blunt edge of a butcher's knife into fire and then pressing it into my flesh. A line for Dornan Ross and a line for each of his six older sons. Notches on a bedpost. Scarred for a lifetime so that I can never forget. Some are thicker than others, some short and others long, but each one a devastating reminder of everything they took from me that night.

Even if I stay in my stale clothes to avoid seeing my scars, I still can't escape them. I never sleep well. I toss and turn, fitful and drenched in sweat, awakening from nightmares where they find me and turn the knife to the sharp side. Where they don't just brand me – they cut me until I am dead, so I won't talk to the police. I know things, see. I know things that the police don't, about purchased alibis and body disposal spots, about too many girls who went missing and too many men who kept too many secrets.

I used to wish every day and every night to forget about my father's murderer and what he did to us. Not anymore. Now I want to remember every tiny detail so that I can exact my revenge.

Tomorrow is different. Tomorrow is my twenty-first birthday, the day I gain access to my secret inheritance. The several hundred thousand that my father managed to hide before Dornan framed him for the murder of a policeman and his family, a crime that Dornan and his eldest son committed as retribution for a drug bust that almost wiped the club out. It might be dirty money – my father wasn't above money laundering and drug manufacturing – but it was *his* money. Dornan managed to seize control of the rest when he enacted his devastating betrayal.

Tomorrow is truly my birthday, for I will become another person. Today my name is Juliette Portland, but tomorrow I will wake up as someone else entirely.

Someone who will bring Dornan Ross and the Gypsy Brothers Motorcycle Club to their knees.

TWO

I'VE NEVER LEFT THE COUNTRY before, but I'm not worried. The night of my twenty-first birthday, I don't party, but arrive in Thailand after a long and cramped flight from the U.S. I have lost time, and it is already morning in Bangkok. I travel directly to the hospital where I will be having my procedure – this isn't a sightseeing holiday, after all. I'm not here for fun.

I'm here to be reborn.

The staff are efficient and discreet. I am admitted and the surgeon goes over the final computer-enhanced photographs which show what I'll look like *after.*

Before the surgery, I go into the private ensuite and strip down. I have a moment of unexpected sadness as I study myself one last time. I've already colored my strawberry blonde hair a deep chestnut brown, but apart from that, this is how I was born. I look exactly like my mother. Tall, skinny, no boobs, green eyes. A light smattering of freckles across my nose is the only thing I got from my father, and a laser is about to burn them off forever. My nose, once regal and thin, now sits crooked, thanks to Dornan breaking it six years ago. It never healed properly, and it is the main reason I cannot stand my own appearance.

But now, standing here like this, so completely naked and alone, I shed a single tear. For my father. For the little girl I used to be, who had everything ripped away.

I shed a tear because she is about to die, six years after she cheated death.

I wipe the tear away and put on my blue hospital gown, tying it at the back. Leaving the cubicle, I enter the room where my procedures will be performed. Twelve hours is all it will take to make me into a completely new person – a new nose, new skin, porcelain veneers on my teeth, fuller cheekbones, and new boobs. I wanted them to remove the scars on my hip, but the laser regimen would take months against all that messy scar tissue. Instead, I'll get a tattoo when I'm back in the States.

As I lay down on the operating table, a nurse hovers over me, a mask in her hand. Before she can lower it, the doctor motions for her to wait.

"Last chance," he says to me. "Are you sure you want to go through with this?" He is an excellent surgeon, and from what I have gleaned, a kind family man. Although he is Asian, he reminds me of my father. There is a patriarchal kindness in his eyes that I haven't seen in a long time.

"Positive," I say, gesturing for the nurse to lower the mask.

"You're going to look beautiful," the surgeon says, and a few moments later, everything goes black.

IT TAKES ME TWO WEEKS to recover enough from the surgery to move around freely, and one month before I resemble a regular human being. I spend my time poolside at the most expensive hotel in Bangkok, attended by nurses who check on my healing wounds and waiters who serve me drinks with umbrellas.

The entire time, I seethe inside, the same way I have seethed for the past six years. What was born as fear and grief has long since blossomed into hatred and rage. Five weeks after my surgery, I return to the USA, hail a cab at LAX, and direct the driver to Venice Beach.

Finally, after six long years, I will have my revenge.

IT'S HOT, AND I CAN feel sweat beads starting to gather between my new breasts. It's funny, I'm still getting used to actually having something decent on my chest. It kind of sucks not being able to sleep on my front, though. Once this is all over, I'm definitely getting them reduced.

For now, I'm a DD cup. Because I know exactly what Dornan "Prez" Ross likes, and it's brunettes with big titties and tanned skin. I am actually surprised that he even bothered raping me. The old me definitely wasn't his type.

I stand out the front of Va Va Voom, the strip joint owned and run by the club, just a few blocks from the Gypsy Brothers clubhouse. When my father was alive, Va Va Voom was actually an upmarket burlesque club. No lap dancing. No hookers out the back. No filth. Dornan changed all that after he had my father murdered.

I push the door open, dragging my small suitcase behind me. It contains everything I'll need for my burlesque show audition. Costumes, some props, my makeup. I have been dancing in my darkened bedroom in Nebraska for years, practicing for this exact moment in time.

The club is dark and smells like stale beer mixed with cheap perfume, with an undertone of dishwasher steam. It's Thursday. Several staff members mill around the bar at one end of the large, open club space, and attractive women in singlets and denim cut-offs practice their dance steps and gossip up on stage. The middle of the place is deserted, and I stand in the center of the cavernous room, my past throbbing in my head like a bullet wound seeping blood. I glance again at the stage and remember what happened there six years ago.

"*Come on, darlin',*" *Dornan laughed, pushing me into the circle formed by six of his sons. The eldest, Chad, caught me by my shoulders and spun me around so that I was facing everyone but him.*

"*Well, aren't you looking mighty fine,*" *Maxi, the third brother, said, wolf-whistling his appreciation. His eyes raked up and down my body and I cringed, looking at the floor. He reached out and slapped me on the ass, making me yowl in surprise. I was terrified. I was fifteen.*

"*Do you understand why you're here, darlin'?*" *Dornan asked me, malice in his black eyes. I shook my head, and returned my gaze to the scuffed wooden stage below my feet. I'd never been here before without my father, and even then I had only ever been here with him after the club was closed, if he needed to pick something up from the office upstairs or drop off a set of keys for whoever was closing up.*

There was a video camera set up at the edge of the stage, pointed towards the circle of men. I smelled their sweat and leather and fought not to cry.

Because, even though I was only fifteen years old and a complete virgin, I knew what came next.

I shook my head no.

Dornan laughed and squeezed my chin between his thick fingers, forcing my head up. He pointed to the camera and brushed a tear from my ashen cheek. He leaned in close so that only I could hear him.

"*Say hello to the camera,*" *he whispered in my ear. "I'm gonna make you a star.*"

I scan the length of the bar, looking for any familiar faces. Any of the Ross brothers or their bastard father. There is no one from six years ago. Just a lone guy, who looks about my age, polishing beer glasses behind the counter. I take a moment to appreciate his fine arms as I cross the room. He's really tall, well over six foot, and hot to boot. His arms both feature full tattoo sleeves. His face is a study in contradictions. He has the sexiness and spunk of a man, with his large brown eyes, thick, beautifully shaped eyebrows and olive-toned skin. His lips are full and wide, and I think for a split second what they would be like to kiss. He has cut his dark brown hair close to his skull. All of this is juxtaposed with the look in his eyes that screams "boy", a look of innocence and naivety.

He looks vaguely familiar, but I'm not worried that he will recognize me. I've studied profiles of every active member of the Gypsy Brothers MC Venice Beach chapter and he hasn't featured.

"Can I help you?" he says, his deep voice like honey and butter.

I plaster a fake smile on and stand a little straighter. My boobs are practically bursting out of my tiny singlet, but he doesn't even give them a cursory glance. He isn't pinging my gaydar, though, so perhaps he's just a gentleman.

"I'm looking for Mr Ross," I say sweetly, delivering my words with a slight southern twang. One highlight of living in a shithole for the past six years is picking up the accent. I don't want to risk anyone recognizing my voice. "I've got an audition."

"Wait here." He turns, giving me a chance to appreciate his ass and...

My heart freezes for a second when I see he's got the Gypsy Brothers family crest on the back of his neck. The crest that's reserved exclusively for the club president, his brothers, and his sons.

Oh fuck. Is he...?

My worst fears are confirmed when he stops at the top of the stairs that lead into the office and shouts into the ajar door, "Pop! Some chick here to see you about a job."

Of course, it's him. Jason Ross. Dornan's youngest son. I almost choke as I remember the last time I saw him.

The boy was screaming. Two of his older brothers held him firmly as he struggled futilely against them.

7

"Are you going to take your turn, son?" Dornan addressed his youngest son. Jase had only been in the care of his father for a very short time – less than a year – and he had struggled to adjust to the MC way of life after his mother's death. Everyone thought that Dornan had been the one to inject Jase's mother with a deadly overdose of heroin – the woman had been clean for sixteen years, since she discovered she was pregnant with Jason and left the club life to raise her son in normality.

I remember lying on the ground, splinters digging into my naked back, wishing I could just die already. Dornan and his six older sons had all taken turns – some, several turns – and my body was dangerously close to shutting down. I had been beaten within an inch of my life, I could taste blood in my mouth from where Dornan had broken my nose, and I was throbbing so badly between my legs it felt like someone was trying to rip me in half.

I had never gone past second base before. It had been a gruesome and devastating way to lose my virginity –to have it stolen.

I watched through blood-encrusted eyelashes as baby-faced Jase fought against his father, even as he knew he would pay dearly for it.

"Please, Pop, please don't, they're hurting her, please stop, STOP STOP STOP!"

"Come on, son," Dornan growled, and I heard the click of a gun being cocked. "Be a man."

Oh God, I remember thinking. This is it. They are going to kill me.

I would have felt pity for Jason, had I not been close to blacking out from the pain.

I whimpered as something cold and metallic was forced between my chattering teeth. Dornan had his gun in my mouth.

I cowered in anticipation. This was it. He was going to shoot me, and I was going to die.

"You better get your dick out and fuck this little bitch, or I'm going to shoot her in the face. Do you understand, son?"

I was listening, but I was floating away at the same time. Little white spots started to appear in my vision as the unbearable pain began to recede.

Jase lunged at his father and I heard a crash, followed by a scuffle and yelling. It was getting hard to hear, though. Everything was turning white and I floated away on that whiteness, relieved to finally be coming to the final moments of my suffering.

"Pop," I heard Chad say. "Pop!"

"What?!" Dornan roared.

"I think she's dying."

"Bullshit." Rough hands shook my body, and there was swearing and jostling as I was picked up and carried.

The world turned white, and then it turned dark as I drifted peacefully away.

When I awoke, the world was not white, but a depressing beige. The pain crept up and socked me hard in the stomach, winding me. I tried to sit up and failed miserably. Some of my ribs were definitely broken.

I felt a warm hand in mine and looked next to me, expecting my mother. Instead, I saw a nightmare that I thought I had woken from.

A scream died in my throat as Dornan gestured with a finger to his lips for me to remain silent. I never even considered defying him, I was so terribly afraid.

"The police would like to talk to you," Dornan said gravely. "I told them my dear niece was going to need some time alone with family first." I stared at him in disbelief, disgusted at what he was implying. Uncle Dornan, posing as a fucking hero in the wake of my father's absence.

I tried to wrench my hand away but he squeezed tighter, cutting off the circulation and forcing a gasp from me.

"What are you going to tell them, Julie, baby?"

I slumped against the bed, defeated. "Nothing."

"I didn't hear you."

"Nothing!" I said a little louder, and snatched my hand back as he released his grip.

"Good," he said, standing up and straightening his leather cut. "I'd hate to have to do to your mother what we did to you."

I cringed at his not-so-subtle threat and shuddered as he planted a kiss on my forehead. "Don't act like the victim," he whispered in my ear. "I know you loved it."

He plastered a fake smile on, tossed a bunch of flowers on the bed next to me, and left the room.

It was the last time I saw him.

And, ironically, the thing that had burned at me the most, more than the betrayal, was the reasoning. I wanted to know why. But then, Dornan murdered my father two days later, shot him in the head at point-blank range with a shotgun. Blew his head clean off.

After that, after Elliot told me my father was dead, I stopped wondering why.

Jase comes back down the stairs, taking them two by two, as if he's in a hurry to be away from the office. He returns to his spot behind the bar and picks up his polishing cloth. "He'll be down soon." I don't answer straight away, and he looks at me from beneath those gorgeous black eyelashes that I used to tease him about. I must look dreadful, because he jerks his head up and frowns.

"Are you okay?"

I nod my head slowly, gripping the bar with both hands.

"Are you sure?" He lifts the cut-out section of the bar counter and comes around to where I am, a glass of iced water appearing in his hand as if by magic.

"You look like you're about to pass out," he says, placing the water on a cardboard coaster in front of me. He brings a bar stool over and sets it down behind me.

I take the water and the seat gratefully, my entire body suddenly aching and tired.

You knew there was a chance you would see him. You knew this was part of the deal.

I shrug and take a sip of water, attempting to pull myself together. If my plan is going to work, I have *got* to keep it together.

"It must be the sun," I say, smiling innocently. "I'm not used to this heat." I hope he doesn't ask me where I'm from. Nebraska is even hotter than California. I feel my story already beginning to crumple under the weight of its artifice.

"Well, take it easy," he says, going back to his side of the bar.

"Thank you," I say meekly, the words tasting like bitter lies on my tongue.

Dornan appears a short time later at the top of the stairs, whistling loudly. "Come on up," he says, beckoning to his office beyond. I look around, unsure if he is even speaking to me.

"Yes, you. Hurry up, I ain't got all goddamn day." He disappears past the doorway and I slide off my stool. I take a deep breath. This is my moment of truth.

This is my one shot to get onside with Dornan and bring this motherfucking family to its shattered kneecaps.

THREE

HE IS SOMEHOW LESS FRIGHTENING than I remember him, and I have to remind myself that I'm taller and stronger than I was when I was fifteen. Back then, I was still so young. Plus, I'm wearing ridiculous heels which make me even taller. Dornan sits behind a desk – my father's old desk – and sifts through paperwork, seemingly oblivious to the fact that I'm standing there. I use the time to take in my surroundings. Nothing special – a generic particle-board desk, a dead pot plant, a couple of tall metal filing cabinets behind the desk. The only item that looks expensive is the painting on the wall, a beach scene that looks like it's from Hawaii or someplace equally beautiful. It doesn't fit in with the room at all, and I wonder if it once belonged to my father.

"Looking for the safe, sweetheart?"

I snap my attention back to Dornan, who is smirking as he pounds numbers into a calculator with his long, thick fingers.

"Looking for the stage," I say, trying to lighten the mood. My entire plan hinges on him hiring me as a dancer for the club. If he doesn't, I'll have to go to plan B. Which I haven't thought of yet.

He leans back in his chair and surveys me properly for the first time. I wait patiently, knowing that I tick all of his boxes – brunette, tanned, big tits and young enough to fuck and employ without getting arrested for employing a minor in the club. I bat my eyelashes and study his face. He is older now, but still bears the strong features that made each of his seven sons unmistakably his. He had no daughters, and that could only be a small mercy fate had delivered.

"What's your name, darlin?" he asks finally, apparently satisfied with my looks. He is still just as blatantly attractive as he was six years ago. Black hair. Wide, sensual lips. Three days growth on his face that makes him look tough and rugged, but not unattractively so. My stomach sinks as I realize that I was wrong, that he and Jase are actually strikingly similar in looks.

"Astrid," I answer, feeling like my heart is about to pound out of my chest.

"Not your stage name," he says, looking irritated. "Your real name."

"Samantha. Sammi."

He looks unimpressed. "You twenty-one?"

I nod. "Twenty-two, actually."

"You got ID to prove that?"

I nod, sliding my fake ID out of my back pocket and handing it to him. I fight back the urge to flee as my fingers brush against his.

He leans back in his chair and studies the small rectangular card. I know he is looking for signs it's a fake. He holds it up to the light, turns it over in his palm, and scrapes his thumbnail along the edge.

"It's real," I say. He doesn't respond.

"What'd you say your name was, again?"

"Sammi. Samantha Peyton."

"Two first names?" he says dubiously. "Who has two first names?"

I smile. "I don't know, Mr. *Ross*. It is a little strange."

He smirks, the closest thing to a smile he's cracked since he called me up here. "Well, Sammi two-first-names Peyton, what kind of job are you looking for?"

I can't believe I'm saying this. "What kind of job do you want me to do?"

He drops the smile. "I'm a busy man. Let's cut to the chase. You dance?"

I nod.

"You do private dances?"

I nod.

"You do anything else that sets you apart from the other hundred girls who come here each week looking for a job?"

I smile wickedly. "I can dislocate my jaw so my mouth opens real wide."

He laughs and slaps the desk in front of him, sending the papers spilling over the side.

"I like you," he decides. "So why here? I mean, I'm sure you know about our... reputation."

I try to look young and helpless. "I just got out of a bad relationship," I say. "Back home in Texas. I could use the protection you offer your employees."

He sucks on his lip, mulling that over.

"Your ex," he says. "Is he a member of any rival motorcycle clubs? A cop? Links to anyone I should be aware of?"

I shake my head. "No."

"You positive about that?"

I nod. "Yeah. He's just an asshole who thinks he owns me."

He nods, apparently satisfied with my act. "You wanna dance first or fuck first?" he asks casually.

I grin from ear to ear, because I'm in. And I know it.

"Mr Ross," I say, leaning over the desk so that my tits are inches from his face, "after I fuck you, it won't matter how well I dance."

Dornan slides past me as he shuts and locks the door, making sure to brush his hardness against my ass as he squeezes past. There is plenty of room behind me and it's completely unnecessary that he even needs to touch me as he walks past, but he obviously feels the need to assert his domination over me. He stands behind me as I face the desk and I can feel his warm breath on my shoulder.

"Turn around," he commands, and I do. He's standing so close to me, I can feel the heat radiating from him in the already stuffy room. His pupils are dilated and he's clearly excited by me.

"Shirt off," he commands, and I oblige, whipping it over my head so that I am wearing nothing but my tiny cut-off shorts and a scrap of lace that cost way more than a bra of that size should. I unhook my bra and let it fall to the ground between us.

"Nice," he says, cupping a breast in each hand. "Not real, though."

I shrug. "I doubt any of your dancers have real ones."

He smirks, and I shudder inwardly. *I'm going to make you a star.*

"Shorts," he says, tugging at the frayed denim that hugs my thighs. It is at this moment that I panic.

Oh, fuck.

My hip bone. The scars. I really hadn't been expecting to have to screw him right here in the office, not today. I had expected to come in, talk business, and come back to audition at night when the stage was set for the rest of the dancers. I know what will happen if he sees it.

He'll kill me.

And this will all be for nothing.

He can see my hesitation and steps back.

"You sure you can handle this kind of work?" he asks me, obviously unimpressed.

I smile tightly. "Of course. I just wasn't expecting it to be today."

"You gonna fuck better next week?" he asks impatiently.

"No," I say quickly. I turn around, shimmy out of my shorts and panties so that I am completely naked, and place my palms flat against the desk. I turn my head to see Dornan watching me with what appears to be a mixture of lust and intrigue.

"I was just thinking," I shrug, flashing him a wicked grin, "I should show you my best stuff straight off the bat."

He laughs and slaps my bare ass with his open hand, squeezing a handful of flesh.

He leans close to my ear, tugging a handful of my long brown hair, forcing my head back. "What do you want from me?" he asks quietly.

I think of how he ruined my life, how he ripped my father from me, how he took my virginity and shared it with his equally sick bastard offspring. I think of the past six years, of staying hidden, of fearing for my life, and I set my jaw squarely.

I want to make you suffer.

"I want you to make me a star," I say sweetly. *I want to bury you alive, you murdering fucking asshole.*

He grins. "Now *that* I can do."

I turn back to the desk and take a deep breath.

"Well, come on, then," I say, grinding myself against his hardness. "Before I change my mind."

I hear a zipper, and feel his fingers as they explore my pussy. "You don't get to change your mind with me."

I squeeze my eyes shut and bite down on my lip, tasting blood as he spits on his hand, using it to lube his cock. I tense as I feel the tip of his shaft press against my opening.

I moan in pain as he shoves his cock deep inside my ass and groans loudly.

"Thought you liked it this way, sweetheart," he says, his balls slapping against skin as he gains speed with his strokes. Each time he pulls out, he thrusts back in with such force, I want to cry.

"I love it," I whisper, hating every second of it.

I force myself to keep up the act, thankful that he won't see my tell-tale branding, and vow to get a tattoo to cover my stupid fucking scars first thing tomorrow morning.

I gasp as I feel a finger press against my clit, and despite my hatred, my traitorous body responds, melting like butter in the midday sun. I suck in a breath as he continues to pleasure me, and I feel my inner resistance fraying and weakening with every swirl of his fingertip. My ass is a cataclysm of pleasure and pain, and the way he is thrumming his fingers against my clit is making me dangerously close to coming.

I am defenceless against his skilled hands as he brings me to the crest of climax, a bitter war waging within me.

Because it shouldn't feel this good.

I moan, bucking my hips against his as my body betrays me completely, greedy for that climax, eager for release.

"Baby girl," Dornan moans, as I explode into a million pieces underneath his deft fingers. That must turn him on, because just as my core clenches and I come, Dornan pulls out of me, stays completely still for a moment, and then groans *that* groan, pushing my face against the desk and spilling hot cum all over my lower back.

I force myself to stay perfectly still, my legs shaking slightly because I've been on my tiptoes, my cheek pressed against the cool desk, because if I don't, I'll scream. I'll scream and claw at his eyes and try to rip them out.

And I can't. I can't just end it all, especially now that I've let him inside me again.

He puffs, catching his breath, his hands still loose around my hips. I lean awkwardly over the desk, mindful that if I stand up straight I'll make a mess on the floor. Dornan reaches for a box of tissues on the desk and wipes his sticky fluid from my skin.

"Thanks," I murmur, turning around to face him, my arm precariously covering my hip. He definitely looks more relaxed than when I first arrived, though he looks tired, too. Too many late nights. Too much blood on his hands. Too many innocent lives, ended at his will.

He strokes my breasts, seemingly absent-minded. I want to push him away, to grab the silver letter-opener from his desk and jam it straight into the family crest on the back of his neck.

"You can clean up in there," he says, pointing to the bathroom that adjoins the office. "Take a shower if you want."

I'll be taking a shower. The hottest fucking shower ever to burn your touch off my skin.

"I'll be quick," I say, high-tailing it into the bathroom with my clothes still held over my torso, covering my scars. I close the door, fighting an inner battle as to whether I should lock the door or not. In the end I don't, but I pull my shorts on immediately, not bothering with the shower. I immediately feel better once they're zipped up and the marred flesh on my hipbone is covered. I grab a towel from the shelf and run it under the faucet until the water is warm, adding a squirt of soap to the material. I wash my back as best I can. I just need to be presentable enough to get back to my hotel before I give myself third-degree burns in the privacy of my own shower.

I put my bra and t-shirt back on and look at myself in the large mirror that hangs over the sink.

A complete stranger stares back at me, so different I wouldn't recognize her as me. Juliette had shoulder-length blonde hair, pale skin, and green eyes. The girl I'm staring at has dark brown hair that skims her ass, thanks to extensions, bronzed skin, thanks to hours lying in a tanning bed, and dark blue eyes that still reflect the tiniest hint of hazel that the contact lenses can't stifle.

I miss being Juliette. But I feel invigorated by my new appearance at the same time. The anonymity it affords me is something I underestimated when Dr. Lee and I were going over my surgical rework plans. I'm on an adrenalin high; having just screwed Dornan, my ass is throbbing but my spirit is elated.

I did it. I fucking did it. I fooled him.

He has no idea who I am.

FOUR

When I exit the bathroom, Dornan is back behind his desk as if nothing ever happened.

"So," I say, as if I don't already know. "Did I get the job?"

He stabs the air with his pen, gesturing for me to sit down. I drag out the metal stool from under the desk — the desk we just fucked on — and sit my throbbing ass down.

"You into drugs?" Dornan asks. "Drinking? What's your thing?"

I shrug. "I'm kind of boring, really."

Dornan smiles knowingly, and flashes his straight teeth. He and his sons might be rough and tattooed, but they all have amazingly straight, white teeth.

"Well," I say, shifting uncomfortably in my seat, "I have a lot of sex with a lot of different people. Could that be a problem?"

His smile stretches so wide I think his face might break under the weight of it. "I don't see that being a problem, no."

"I do have one other problem," I say, looking at the floor. "I mean, I just got here from Texas, I don't know anyone ... I'm staying at a backpackers' hostel a few blocks away, but I'm going to run out of cash soon."

He nods. "You need cash?"

I shake my head. "I don't take money unless I earn it. I just need … somewhere to stay, a few weeks at the most."

Say it, Dornan. Come on and fucking say it.

"That's not a problem," he says, waving his hand dismissively. "You'll stay at the clubhouse. Plenty of extra rooms. You'll have to sign a non-disclosure statement and agree not to speak with anyone about what goes on there, of course."

Hooked, line and sinker. *Sucker.*

"What goes on there?" I say, my Bambi eyes as wide as I can stretch them.

"Baby girl," he replies, clearly high-fiving himself for his luck today. "Why don't you just see for yourself?"

He writes the address down on the back of a business card and hands it to me, letting his fingers brush against mine again. I see the glazed look in his eyes and a small burst of adrenalin spurts into my stomach as I realize he's pretty damn taken with Samantha Peyton.

"Here," he says, handing me a roll of crisp fifties. There's probably cocaine on them. "Get yourself some nice clothes. Damn, I like those shorts, but you gotta wear something a little more upmarket if you're gonna be working here."

I laugh to myself, thinking that he still holds his club to such a high esteem even though he's turned it from an artistic burlesque club to a strip club and whore house.

The cell phone on his desk vibrates and he gives me one last look up and down. "I gotta take this. Go shopping, get yourself some nice things to wear, and I'll see you here," he points to the address on the business card, "tonight. Be there at eight. We'll go over everything then."

I smile broadly and offer my hand. He looks at it, takes it, and pulls me across the desk. I feel his lips on mine and the only thing I can do is respond. He's a good kisser, even though the feel of his hot tongue in my mouth makes me want to clamp my teeth down and bite it off.

He breaks away and lets go of me.

"I think that's a little more appropriate than shaking hands, don't you think?"

I giggle, licking my lips. "Yes, sir."

His phone continues to buzz angrily. "Eight," he says, answering the phone and holding it to his ear. "Now get that piece of ass out of here before I spend my entire day fucking it." He starts barking things into the phone and I back away, grab my roll-along suitcase, and make my way as quickly and quietly as I can down the stairs.

I pass Jase, who is still polishing beer glasses, but I don't make eye contact. I'm almost at the set of doors, where I can go outside and fill my lungs with fresh air before I have a complete meltdown, when he speaks just behind me.

"Did you get the job?"

I turn slowly, ashamed that he has to look at me like this. Like a *whore*. "Yeah," I reply quietly. "I got the job."

Jase looks intrigued, and I have to wonder if he senses something about me. About us. After all, I might be Samantha now, but before that I was Juliette, the first girl he ever loved.

"What's your name?" he asks me, setting a tray of glasses on a table between us.

Julz! Don't touch her! Get away from her! Juliette!

I turn, swallowing back a lifetime of tears, and smile at him. "Samantha. You can call me Sammi."

He nods. "Well, see you 'round, Sammi."

"Yeah," I say, and suddenly my sadness is so heavy, I'm afraid I might collapse on the floor in front of him. But I don't. I swallow back the hard lump in my throat and turn to leave. "See you 'round."

When I steal a glance over my shoulder as I'm pushing the heavy doors open, he is still watching me.

FIVE

I NEARLY DIDN'T MAKE IT out of LA alive.

If it weren't for Elliot smuggling me out of town and setting me up in Nebraska, I would have been dead that very night I lay in hospital, broken and bleeding. Dornan's second son, Donny, had been on his way back to the hospital to inject a lethal dose of heroin into my veins while Elliot was questioning me.

"Who did this to you?" the young police officer asked softly. I stared into space, unable to form words.

"I'd rather stay alive," I said finally, shaking my head.

He leaned close and whispered to me, so close I could almost taste the coffee on his breath. "It was Dornan Ross, wasn't it?"

The fear that leapt into my eyes must have confirmed his suspicions.

"I think they're planning to kill you whether you tell me or not," he said urgently. "They've been hanging around your room all afternoon, waiting for me to leave."

My entire aching body stiffened, and my heart started beating so fast, I thought it would explode out of my chest and drench the beige walls in a shower of red.

Elliot eyed the small cart in the corner of the room that was meant for washing. He lifted the lid and peered inside, pulling out

*a blood-stained set of green hospital scrubs with his fingertips.
He quickly and efficiently stripped down to his boxers, which
would have been completely traumatising for me had I not
believed that he was trying to help. He dragged the green scrubs
over his head and hopped around, trying to pull the pants on as
quickly as possible.*

*He came back over to the bed and unhooked my IV from the
stand. I had a bag of morphine attached to the main saline bag,
and a little button I could press to deliver a new hit of pain relief
every fifteen minutes.*

*Elliot pressed and held the button, delivering the maximum
dose possible, and almost immediately I felt floaty and numbed.*

*"Scoot forward," he said, looking around behind him. He lifted
me as gently as possible, but I still screamed in pain from my
broken bones being moved. "I'm sorry," he said, covering my
mouth so that no sound escaped.*

*He maneuvered me to the side of the bed so that my legs were
hanging off, and eased me down into the laundry cart. I wriggled
down, biting on my fist to stop from screaming, and arranged
myself so that the lid would close on top of me.*

*"Here," he said, handing me his gun, and that's the moment
when any suspicion I had about his intentions melted away.*

*"If this doesn't work, and somebody else opens this lid ...
shoot and keep shooting, you hear?"*

I nodded.

"You know how to use a gun?"

*I nodded, tears streaming down my cheeks. My father, up until
a few weeks ago, had been the president of the most renowned
and feared biker club in the United States. Of course I knew how
to use a gun.*

"I'm gonna get you out of here, kid. I promise."

And he did.

Six years later, Elliot isn't a cop anymore. In fact, he resigned
from the force almost immediately after moving me to a safe

house in Nebraska with his grandmother. Juliette Portland was reported dead in the hospital from internal bleeding the night he smuggled me out, and while we think that Dornan bought the story, it's always possible that he is still keeping watch for me.

I'm standing outside a building with LOST CITY TATTOOS emblazoned across the front, my dirty clothes switched for a spaghetti-strap white summer dress that skims my knees and shows off my enviable tan. I've just spent the last hour scrubbing every inch of myself in the shower of my hotel room. I wasn't actually staying in a dingy hostel. I had a room at the Bel Air. I figured I may as well enjoy my last few hours of freedom before moving into the clubhouse tonight.

I push the door open and am immediately hit by a breeze of cold air. The air-conditioning is bliss against my reddened skin, which has started to prickle after only a few moments outside. It is so much cooler inside, I think I might never leave.

I am expecting the humming of tattoo guns, but everything is silent. I look around the room, seeing nobody.

"Hello?" I call, waiting for an answer.

"Hi," a voice behind me says, startling me. I spin around to see Elliot, still looking as gorgeous as he did the last time I saw him, only now more grown-up, and with tattoos covering every visible inch of his skin. He wears a white t-shirt and dark grey dickie shorts, a pair of bright blue sneakers on his feet. His face is the only thing that assures me of who he is.

I study his face and wonder if he knows who I am, then decide he probably doesn't. "You don't know who I am, do you?"

He immediately looks suspicious. "No. Should I?"

I shake my head, my fake Southern drawl thick on my words. "It doesn't matter. I came here because I need a tattoo. Everyone says you're the best."

He smiles, licking his lips, and I see a flash that I think is a tongue stud. "Come on through," he says, leading me to one of the hard leather beds. "What kind of tattoo are you after?"

"One to cover a scar," I say, biting my lip.

He nods, patting the bed. I hoist myself up, studying his face intently. *He is the kindest person I have ever met,* I think to myself. He truly did risk his life to save mine.

"Okay," he says, smiling. "Where's your scar?"

I swallow thickly, gather my dress in my fist, and raise it so that he can see.

His face contorts into something tortured. He looks at me, then the scars, then back at me.

"Julz?" he whispers. He takes in my hair, my skin, my blue eyes, my new nose. He steps back as if horrified.

"It's Samantha, now," I say, the accent gone, my breath hitching in my throat. "And I need your help."

SIX

HE DOESN'T SPEAK. DOESN'T MOVE. I suddenly feel ill, as though I have done the wrong thing by seeking him out.

"I'm sorry," I say, pulling my dress back down and sliding off the bed. "I shouldn't have come here."

I try to leave but he catches my elbow, turning me to face him. "Wait," he says. "Please. I don't want you to go. I'm just a little ... shocked. I haven't seen you in three years."

I just stand there, feeling pathetic.

"Juliette," he says darkly. "What are you doing here?"

"Sightseeing," I reply with a deadpan face.

He lets go of my elbow and walks to the front of the store. He flips the sign hanging in the door to closed and locks the door, pulling the shade down so nobody can see in.

"My apartment is upstairs," he says, looking at me like my appearance is causing him physical pain. "I think we need to talk."

"And then you'll tattoo me?" I ask hopefully.

He appears to be fighting an inner battle. "If you tell me why you need *those* scars covered up, then sure, I'll make you the best fucking tattoo you've ever seen."

"I'll tell you why if you promise you won't try and talk me out of it."

He suddenly looks weary. "Let's just go upstairs," he says, "before anyone else finds you here."

I look around the deserted shop, confused as to who exactly is going to find me in a store that is now locked, but I follow him upstairs anyway.

I am pleasantly surprised when I enter the apartment. It is a far cry from the stark white of the store, and feels surprisingly spacious. It has been decorated in a retro style, all black and reds, with hits of canary yellow here and there. There are band posters covering the walls – from a cursory glance, I can see bills for The Ramones, The Rolling Stones and the Red Hot Chili Peppers. Knotted beams of polished oak run beneath my feet. There are two low-back, black leather sofas facing each other with a glass coffee table between them and a gloss-black kitchen tucked off to the side.

Elliot walks behind the bench and reappears several moments later with two open bottles of Budweiser.

"Good idea," I say, accepting the one he offers me.

He sits across from me, and I can't help but remember the very first time I saw him after my father died, when he came back to Nebraska.

I'd been puking. At first, Grandma wrote it off as a stomach virus and kept me in bed for the week. But one week slowly crept into two, then three, and I was still sick, still lying in bed all day, and the doctor eventually confirmed what she had secretly feared and what I had never considered.

I heard her on the phone to her grandson, late one night when I couldn't sleep.

"You have to come back here," she pleaded. "It's bad, honey. It's real bad."

She knew everything. She knew what they had done to me. And now, she knew that I carried a lasting reminder of their treachery.

Elliot was there the next day, sitting beside me as I puked into an old tin bowl. He held my blonde hair back as I vomited, pressed a cold flannel to my neck. He cared for me the way I desperately needed someone to care for me.

"What do you want to do?" he asked me. Even then, when I was only fifteen and he was just shy of twenty-three, he treated me like I was the most important person in the world.

"I just want it to go away," I said. "Can you make it go away?"

He clutched my hand, both of us trapped in a nightmare that never seemed to end.

"Yeah," he said, the rage in his clenched jaw meant for them, not me. "I can make it go away."

We drove to the clinic in silence. He filled out the paperwork for me, used a fake ID so nobody would know my real name.

He held my hand the whole time, as I was counselled, as I was prepped for theater, as the remnants of Dornan's duplicity were painfully sucked from my cramping womb.

He crouched at the foot of my bed as I bled and cried. He stroked my hair and promised me he would kill Dornan Ross and his sons for what they had done to me. That he would make them pay.

For everything.

I shake that horrid memory from my mind and focus on the here and now.

"Are you going to stare at me all day?" I ask him gently, attempting to get a smile.

He slams his beer down on the glass coffee table and froth sloshes onto the wooden floor.

"A goddamned *ghost* just walked into my shop asking for a tattoo," he says gravely. "Excuse me for needing a minute to *deal*."

I look at the floor. "A ghost is someone who died. I didn't die."

"No," he says, shaking his head. "But everyone in this city thinks you did."

I sip on my beer as I study the intricate network of Elliot's tattoos that reach from each wrist to shoulder before disappearing under his shirt.

"Why are you back, Julz?" he asks, studying me intently. My heart drops when I realize his hands are shaking.

"Hey," I say, setting my beer down and putting my hands over his so we are both cupping his beer. "I'm sorry. I didn't mean to scare you."

"Fuck," he says bitterly. "The last time I saw you ..."

"Calm down," I interrupt him. "Nobody knows I'm here, I swear."

I take the bottle from his hands and set it down next to mine, and shift seats so that I am sitting next to him.

"Remember the last thing we spoke about?" I whisper, taking his hands in mine. It's been so many years, but it feels like it was five minutes ago that he was holding my hands like this and promising me vengeance.

He shakes his head. "No."

"Yes, you do," I prod firmly. "You promised me you would make them pay."

His eyes go wide as he finally understands what I'm here for. "Julz, no ..."

"Elliot, yes," I murmur. "It's time. It's time to make them pay for their sins."

He pulls away from me and stands, walking over to the window. It is blessedly cool and dim in the apartment compared to the scorching heat outside. I look at my iPhone, aware that I am supposed to be at the clubhouse in four hours and require a tattoo that will take at least five. Still, I bear the moments as patiently as I can, worried that to push Elliot will make him refuse to help altogether. And, really, I can go to any tattoo artist and request a coverup for my scars.

But in a town run by Dornan Ross, I can't risk showing his macabre handiwork to a single soul. Because if someone finds me out, I'm as good as dead.

And I still have so many things left to do.

"It should have been me taking them down, Julz, not you."

I speak gently. "Grandma told me about your daughter."

He seems startled, fear registering in his eyes.

"What I mean," I say quickly, "is that I understand why you haven't been able to do anything about…" I'm suddenly at a loss for words. "Well, you know."

Elliott rubs his eyes, and I wonder how many sleepless nights he has had since we met in an Emergency Room decorated in beige and bathed in my blood six years ago. Or how many sleepless nights since he drove away and left me all alone, three years ago?

Elliot keeps shaking his head. "You shouldn't have come back," he says. "You should have stayed away."

I rise from the couch. "I have four hours to get a tattoo that covers these scars. I am doing this with or without you. Are you going to help me, or am I going to leave and find another tattoo artist to cover this shit up?"

He turns, seemingly shocked by my determination. "Dornan knows artists all over this city. You can't show your," his voice cracks, "scars around."

"Elliot," I say firmly. "I've dreamed about this for years. I've danced in the dark after the lights were switched off, teaching myself the things I needed to know. I've memorized every single thing about Dornan Ross and committed it to memory. I am doing this with or without your help."

With my final outburst, I turn to leave. I am bluffing, but he doesn't know that. I think of the last time we were together, three aching years ago, and I can't bear to think about how he walked away from me.

It was hot and dusty. It was always fucking hot and dusty. It had been a year since I had "died", since I had been smuggled out of a hospital room circled by men who wanted to kill me, and delivered to a safe house thousands of miles away from everything I had ever known.

Elliot was my one constant. He was gentle and kind. He listened to all of the demons inside me that were clamoring to smother me, to kill me. He held me while I cried. He wiped away my tears.

And then, inexplicably, he fell in love with me.

We waited for a long time to do anything more than fool around, but once we took that final step, I was his, body and soul. I loved him. He was my world.

Only, he wasn't enough to chase away the demons. Nothing was.

For the first three years after I escaped, I was a broken shell, trying to survive, trying to forget. The scars, my constant reminder. The sound of a motorcycle. The touch of leather under my fingertips. Being in confined spaces.

I was broken, destroyed, and although he tried, Elliot couldn't put me back together again.

The first time I tried to kill myself, I swallowed a bottle of pain pills from his grandmother's bathroom cupboard. It didn't work. I woke up and I was still alive.

Elliot begged me to promise I'd never do it again. I did, and then the next day, I hooked up a hose to the exhaust of his car, locked the garage, and waited for sweet release.

Of course, he found me. Cut through the garage door with an ax and saved my sorry ass.

The third time, I was so pathetically obvious that he found me in the bath before I'd even had a chance to drag the razor blade down my wrists.

After the third time, he left. Because I was darkness, and he was sinking inside that darkness, and every time he tried to pull me out, I'd hold him under with me.

I understood. His life had revolved around saving my life for three whole years, and he couldn't save me anymore.

"I have nothing left to give you," is what he said, before he climbed into his car and drove away.

It was only after he'd left me that I realized I had been going about things all wrong.

That it wasn't forgiveness and forgetting that my soul truly craved.

Once I set my sights on vengeance, life made perfect sense.

But by then, it was too late for Elliot and me. Our time was up. He was already with another girl, his baby in her belly.

So I stayed in Nebraska and learned to dance, and dreamed of my revenge.

"WAIT," HE SAYS.

I stop, still staring at the door that will take me downstairs.

He sighs audibly. "I'll do it. If you promise to tell me what you're up to."

I spin around, the smile on my face impossible to fight. "I told you," I say, grinning like an idiot. "I'm going to take them out. Dornan Ross will rot in jail for life, and his sons will suffer, too."

Eliot looks at me quizzically. "The cops have never been able to get anything to stick on Ross OR his sons. What makes you think you're different?'

I laugh. "Well, I'm the dead girl, aren't I? I'm going to find that tape he made of me, and send it to every single TV station in the country. They'll have no choice but to charge him with my murder."

Elliot nods, and a slow, sweet smile spreads across his face. He takes the three steps across his apartment to reach me and pulls me into a bear hug so tight, I can barely breathe.

"I missed you," he says, his arms pressed tight around me.

I think of how we were strangers once, pulled together by circumstance and a burning will to survive. How, even though we haven't laid eyes on each other in so long, Elliot is the one person on this planet who truly understands me and my past.

"Missed you too," I murmur sadly, wishing it didn't have to be like this, but knowing without a shadow of a doubt that *it does*.

SEVEN

FOUR AND A HALF HOURS later, I'm running to the address Dornan gave me. Of course, I don't need to look at the card – I know exactly where the clubhouse is. I'm almost there when it occurs to me that the address looked a little off, and I stop to fish the card out of my bag.

Sure enough, the address on the card is not for the clubhouse at all. I stand under the yellow glow of a street lamp, trying to massage the stitch out of my abdomen without touching the fresh tattoo gouged into my side.

I unlock my iPhone screen and navigate to the maps section. I plug-in the address that Dornan has written down for me, and wait impatiently as it loads. The little red dot is telling me to go in the opposite direction – 200 yards to what appears to be an abandoned warehouse. I jog the 200 yards and come to a stop in front of the warehouse, my fear a living thing inside me. My heart sinks as I wonder why Dornan wants me here instead of down the road at the clubhouse.

I jump suddenly as a dark figure materializes out of the shadows. I immediately recognize him as Jazz, Dornan's fifth son. He is painfully thin, and it doesn't take a genius to realize he has some kind of drug problem.

"Hey, sweetheart," he calls out to me. "What's your name?"

"Sammi," I reply, my heart hammering in my chest.

"You're late," Jazz says, pushing open the enormous old roller door and gesturing inside. "You'd better hurry up and come inside."

I hesitate for a moment, my feet itching for a decision.

Fuck it. I sling my bag over my shoulder, set my jaw, and walk to the doorway, ducking underneath the roller door. I try not to cringe as it is slammed shut behind me, the sudden rush of cold air nipping at my heels.

It is dim inside the warehouse, and I struggle to see more than superficial figures as my eyes adjust to the lighting.

There are figures moving casually about. From what I can see, all male. Before I can make out their faces, Jazz has snatched my bag from my hand and immediately begins rifling through the contents.

"Hey!" I protest. Another set of hands pulls my arm behind my back, forcing it up in a painful V. I am slammed into a brick wall and the wind is knocked right out of my lungs.

Be cool.

I feel hands patting me down, efficiently at first, before slowing down when they reach my inner thighs. I stay perfectly still as someone - who, I have no idea – gently teases my clit as they search me. I don't react.

"Where's Dornan?" I ask. "He told me to meet him here."

"Shut up," another voice says, and I turn to follow its owner. It seems the fingering body search has ended, and I am allowed to move freely again. Dornan's oldest son, Chad, is standing in front of me, my iPhone in his hand.

"What's the password for this thing?" he asks me.

I smirk. "D...I...C..."

I'm about to finish that word when he throws the phone at the ground, so hard it explodes into a million tiny pieces. I look at the ground in disgust and then back up at him.

"Oops," he says, raising his eyebrows for effect. I don't say anything, just hold his gaze without wavering.

"What's your name?" Chad asks, repeating Jazz's earlier question.

If you knew who I was, you'd shoot me in the head right now where I stand.

I look over at Jazz as if to say, *why don't you tell them?* He doesn't speak.

"It's Sammi," I say. "Samantha."

Jazz tosses my purse to Chad, who pulls out my license and studies it intently.

"What's your address?" he asks. I act bored and recite my address perfectly, followed by my date of birth when asked.

"What's your license number?" he asks. I know it, but I also know that most people don't. That it's probably MORE suspicious being able to rattle it off than it is to feign ignorance.

"How the fuck should I know?" I say incredulously, tossing my long hair over my shoulder. "Do you know your license number?"

He laughs and shoves my fake license back into my purse, tossing it to Jazz, who hands it to me along with my bag.

"Where's Dornan?" I repeat. "I'm supposed to start working for him. I don't want to be late."

Dornan steps out of the shadows, and I jump minutely, unaware that he's been watching the entire time.

"Baby girl," he says, his deep voice commanding respect among his sons, who seem to stand to attention all of a sudden. "You're already late."

I smile nervously. "I'm so sorry. The tattoo artist took forever—"

"Tattoo artist?" Dornan cuts me off sharply. "What tattoo artist?"

I shrug. "Some guy near the pier. You wanna see?"

He smiles, and despite my hatred for him, I can definitely understand why so many women throw themselves at him. His deep, booming gravel voice; his unmistakeable good looks that he's inevitably passed on to all of his sons; those coal black eyes that miss nothing and give nothing away. Yes, I can see why he has seven sons to five different women. He's just got *something* I can't quite put my finger on. A charisma, an allure, a larger-than-life presence. Even at forty-eight, he's only getting better looking with age.

It makes me hate him even more.

"Sure," he says. He looks impatient. I smile, lifting my white dress so that he has a clear view of my lace panties, and stick my hip out.

Dornan whistles. "That's some nice ink you got there, sweetheart."

"I got it for you," I say, smiling shyly. "I know all your girls have them."

The sons don't seem impressed. In fact, most of them look downright bored.

It's ironic, really. That, cunning as they all are, they don't realize their judge, jury and executioner stands before them, painted in roses and ink.

My heart *soars* at the thought of what I will do to each of them.

EIGHT

TWENTY MINUTES LATER, WE ARE in Dornan's room at the clubhouse. I know he has a home, but his wife is probably there. *That poor woman.* After my humiliating strip-search, he whisked me away, up here, away from the curious eyes of his sons and fellow club mates. I am equal parts relieved and annoyed. Relieved that I didn't have to put on a show in front of so many suspicious guys, or dance with my bandaged tattoo on full show. Annoyed because I can't breathe properly in this room, large as it is, since the windows all have metal bars on them and I am unmistakably trapped. Alone. With *him.*

My scars are hidden nicely by Elliot's handiwork, but if someone knew what they were looking for, if they studied my skin long enough, they would find them.

"You understand why I had to have my boys search you before you could come in here, right?"

I stretch out on his bed, resting on my elbows and attempting to look unperplexed. "Of course. You don't want some crazy bitch coming in here."

"Or a cop," he says, looking at me sidelong through his thick eyelashes. Christ, his voice is so deep, I can *feel* everything he is saying rumble through me like a freight train.

"When am I going to dance?" I ask him. I'm not enjoying being cooped up in a room alone with him, and I'm craving fresh air.

He smiles menacingly, and my stomach drops as I remember I don't have my phone anymore. That idiot smashed it right after his brother finger-fucked me. *Shit.*

"You're not going to dance," he says.

"Oh," I say, acting a little disappointed. "You want me to waitress or something instead? Because I could show you my routine–"

He kneels in front of me so that his face is inches from mine. I can smell mint on his breath and some kind of aftershave mixed in with his sweat. It's not offensive, except that it's *his*.

"I haven't stopped thinking about you all afternoon," he says, walking his fingers up my thighs. I smile naughtily at him as he threads a finger inside my panties, searching.

I fidget as he finds my pussy and inserts one finger, then two, then pushes three in. I can't help it. I moan as he applies the slightest pressure to my clit with the pad of his thumb. I can't keep looking at him, I need to close my eyes, so I pull his face to mine, our lips crashing together in a kind of frenzy.

He takes his hand away and tugs at my dress, taking it over my head before throwing it to the floor. I wince as he lightly traces the intricate patterns of roses and a phoenix rising from the ashes that now adorns my midsection.

"Need to be inside you, baby girl," he moans, unbuttoning his jeans and letting his hardness rise to full size. I have a chance to study it more closely. Yup. No wonder my ass is so sore. His cock is *huge*.

He doesn't even bother taking my panties off, just pushes them to the side with rough, crazed hands. I am equal parts thrilled and terrified that I have had this effect on him in the space of a few short hours. I think briefly of my makeover and mentally high-five myself for getting everything completely right.

He pushes me down on the bed, hovering his cock between my thighs.

"You're mine now," he says, thrusting inside me with enough force to make me cry out. He immediately starts pumping in and out, hard and fast, and my brain does battle with my body. So many conflicting emotions are vying for my attention, I am completely and utterly overwhelmed.

Ohhhh.

I open my eyes to see him above me and am immediately a scared, bleeding fifteen-year-old girl again.

No. Don't think about that. Pretend he's someone else. *Remember why you're here.*

And that delicious knowledge of my deceit stirs something carnal in my belly, a snaking kind of desire that coils around me and squeezes tightly. *Yes. Better.*

I reach up and wrap my arms around his neck, the thrill of my treachery almost enough to make me orgasm on its own.

"That feels so good," I moan, and he smirks because he thinks he is fucking me, when I am the one fucking him.

He is a skilled lover. I don't have anyone to compare him to, other than my high-school sweetheart from Nebraska, but as he carries me to the brink of climax on a white-hot wave of pleasure and lies, I cannot help but scream.

Afterwards, we lie together, catching our breath. I look at him out of the corner of my eye to see him staring back.

"Where've you been my whole life, baby?" he asks, running his hands over my breasts and between my legs. His touch is everywhere, all over me, marking me as his, a possession that has been claimed.

I smile coyly. "In high school, probably," I giggle.

"Hey, now," he replies playfully. "Don't tell me I gotta prove to you that age doesn't matter?"

"I think you just did," I breathe.

We lie there in silence for a few blessed moments. It gives me time to think. Time to plan.

Dornan's voice strikes that silence, shattering my moment of refuge.

"I just have one question for you, baby girl."

One question. Sounds easy. I turn to face him and nod in anticipation.

"Your ex. What was his name?"

It's one teeny, tiny white lie. "Michael," I say, my fake backstory flashing before my fake blue eyes. "Michael Trevine."

He nods. "He'll never hurt you again. Why won't he hurt you again?"

I smile dreamily, imagining the look on his face when they put him in orange overalls and slam his jail cell shut forever. Maybe they'll give him the death penalty.

They should.

"Because," I say playfully, tracing his lips with my finger, "I'm yours?"

He just fucking laughs. "What have I done to deserve you?" he breathes.

Now *I* am the one who laughs.

NINE

I GREW UP NEXT TO the ocean. Until I was fifteen years old, I had no idea that some people could go an entire lifetime without ever seeing the sea.

And then, one night, I was forced to flee from it, ripped from its beauty forever.

I didn't see a beach for six years. Landlocked and bitter, surrounded by dirt and storms and nightmares of Dornan Ross's face.

So when I wake up, after barely sleeping, to see his unshaven face peering down at me, it is all I can do not to scream.

"Whoa," he says, grinning like the cat that got the motherfucking cream. "Bad dream?"

I sit up, pushing the sheets off me to discover I am completely naked, my tattoo angry and red and burning. Elliot warned me about this. But instead of trying to avoid thinking about the pain, I relish it. The burn helps me to remember why I am here.

It makes me remember how good it feels to be alive.

"Good morning," I say, rubbing my eyes. I lean back, letting my breasts jut out in full view so that he can see them. "Oh Jesus," he says, groaning loudly. I can see the bulge in his pants. The man is literally ready to go any time of the day.

"Wish I could stay, baby girl," he says, handing me a mug of hot black coffee. "But I gotta go run a job with my boys."

"That's okay," I say, arranging the sheets around myself. "I've got to go and get this tattoo finished, anyway."

"Oh, you're not going anywhere," he says. I almost choke on my coffee.

"P-pardon?" I ask, wiping coffee from my chin.

"Severe storm warning's in place," he says, shoving his wallet into the back pocket of his jeans. "I've got about ten minutes before this motherfucking weather outside becomes damn near impossible to drive in. Lucky we weren't planning to ride."

"So, you want me to stay here?" I ask. "By myself?"

He drains his own coffee cup. "Nope. My son's gonna be here. Jase. He's staying behind with you." He looks at me oddly for a moment, and I can't tell what he's thinking. "Besides, little runt is the only one of the lot that I'd trust to take care of your fine ass." He leans closer and smiles conspiratorially. "I'm eighty percent sure he's gay. Don't tell anyone, though. Little fucker'd be beaten to death by his brothers if anyone else knew."

Jase. *Fuck.*

I just smile vacantly, my mind going a million miles an hour. I'm essentially trapped, without a phone or a way out. I memorized Elliot's number, but that doesn't actually matter if I haven't got a way of calling him. And I don't want to raise any suspicions by making a big deal of contacting him.

I just pray he doesn't get impatient and report me missing. Especially since, technically, I'm already dead.

"Okay," I say brightly. "Where are you going?"

Dornan chuckles as he pulls his leather cut on over his black t-shirt. My throat gets tight as I see the club colors adorning the black leather, the *President* badge unmissable. It is exactly like the jacket my father used to wear.

"It's a surprise, babe. You'll see soon enough."

A surprise. I wonder what the fuck *that* could possibly be. I have to strain forcibly to stop my eyes from rolling violently back into my head.

"I like your jacket," I say softly. "It looks comfy."

He puffs his chest out and studies himself in the mirror next to the bed. "I got it when I became president of this club," he says, and something inside of me dies a little. So it *is* my father's jacket.

"Get dressed," Dornan says, still preening himself in front of the mirror. I obey, swinging my legs out of the bed. I find my bag next to the bed and select a new outfit – dark denim jeans and a white halter top that exposes my cleavage nicely. I pull on the jeans and halter, then make my way into the adjoining bathroom to apply some more mascara and fix my bed hair.

Ten minutes later, I am being paraded around in front of the club members who are still at the club. We are downstairs in the main room, which features lots of low-back leather couches, a fully-stocked bar that we stand in front of, and a small stage at one end. There are no windows, which makes me itch. I know why. Windows mean people can see inside. Windows mean people can shoot bullets through.

I look around, scanning the dozen or so guys and girls hanging off Dornan's every nauseating word. I guess most people have decided to return home after the storm warning was issued. I tune in to what Dornan is saying as he's finishing up.

"Nobody is to touch her," he finishes. "She's mine. You hear?"

I smile vacantly as a few guys jostle and wolf-whistle and a few slutty-looking girls look seethingly jealous as they look me up and down.

Dornan snaps his fingers and grabs my arm. "Come on," he says. "Time for me to go." I trot after him like an obedient puppy, taking in every detail I can about the place.

Some things have changed, and some have stayed exactly the same. Dornan is still an asshole – that definitely hasn't changed.

I follow him out of the main club room, down a narrow hallway that has several closed doors and which eventually opens up into a large kitchen, complete with several dining tables.

"Wait here," he says, stabbing a table with his finger. I sit at the table and look up at him. "What am I waiting for?"

He leans on the side of the table and studies my face. "We're just waiting, that's all."

I nod, looking around the room. Photos of club members dot the walls, and my throat catches when my gaze lands squarely on a photo I remember well. A photo I've been carrying around for six years. My copy now lies in a safety deposit box under another fake name in downtown LA.

My father.

I force myself to look away, certain Dornan is studying me. He may have allowed me into his club, but I know damn well that he still doesn't trust me an inch.

Jase hurries into the room a few moments later, looking as though he's just stepped out of a shower fully dressed. He's creating a water slick behind him and when he stops in front of his father, that slick becomes a full-fledged puddle.

"Jesus fucking Christ," Dornan says, towering over his son even though they are both about the same height.

"You're making a goddamned mess, boy."

Jase wipes the moisture from his face and more droplets of water rain down. I have to force myself not to smile. Jase clearly enjoys making his father upset.

"I had to ride through the rain. It's crazy out there."

It is only now that I realize he's carrying a black motorcycle helmet in one hand, the chin strap looped over his fingers.

Dornan shakes his head. "Borrow a fucking car next time," he says. "I don't need you dyin' out there."

Jase nods. "Why'd you call me down? I thought you wanted me in the club today."

Dornan shifts so that Jase can see me. Jase immediately looks unimpressed.

"I gotta go on a run for a day or two," Dornan says. "I need you to keep this one company for me."

"This one?" Jase asks caustically. "Isn't *this one* supposed to be working tonight?"

Dornan looks from me to his son and sighs. "Look, boy, I don't have time to get into it now. She's something special, you hear? I've decided she's better off here at the club, keeping your old man company."

I am dying to speak, but I know Dornan likes his women stupid and obedient, so I keep my mouth shut.

"How long you planning to be gone?" Jase asks, looking generally disinterested.

"Two days, tops," Dornan replies. "Get Kathy to cover you at the club. And son … " He pulls me from my seat by my shoulder and stands me in front of Jase - "I would never let your brothers near Sammi here, you understand?"

Yeah, right, I think to myself.

"But you, son, I know you've had it real hard since Raelene left us. God bless her soul. So if you wanna sample this fine piece of ass," he slaps my ass with his wide hand, "you go right ahead, you hear?"

My whole body jumps a little at being slapped and I look at Dornan questioningly.

Jase is glaring at his father and refuses to look at me or even acknowledge my presence. "I don't need your sloppy seconds," he says to his father, and I want to vomit. This is so much harder, so much more real, than I ever imagined it would be. The way Jase looks at me, when he does look at me, makes me want to scream.

It is a far cry from the guy who offered me a glass of water and a seat yesterday, and nothing at all like the boy who wanted to save me from all of this once upon a time.

The boy who I used to love.

47

"Are you sure you're not one of those fucking faggots?" Dornan asks, clearly pissed off at his son's blatant rejection of what he no doubt considers to be a generous offer.

Jase just rolls his eyes. "I'm sure, Pop. Go on now, before you miss your chance. That storm is a bitch and it's only getting worse."

Lightning cracks on cue overhead and I jump nervously.

"What's wrong with you?" Jase demands.

I hate storms. I fucking hate them with a passion. When I was a little girl, I used to go and hide under my bedcovers and wait for the fury of Mother Nature to pass.

Sometimes, when we were younger, Jase used to hide with me.

"Nothing," I say. "I don't like storms is all."

Jase eyes me curiously, flicking his eyes up and down me. In that moment, I wonder if he is going to guess who I am eventually. He is clever and shrewd, and I am probably only a few careless remarks away from raising his suspicion.

"They make my hair frizz," I add, trying to think of other reasons why people might hate storms. "I have to use my hair straightener, like, three times a day when it's this humid."

Jase looks at me like one might look at a cockroach squashed on the bottom of their shoe. I shrivel inside under the power of his ambivalence.

You used to love me once.

I can't think of those things right now. Maybe not ever.

Dornan pulls me towards him and plants his hands firmly on my ass cheeks.

"Gonna miss you, baby girl," he says, sucking hard at my neck so that I gasp. He's a grown man giving me a fucking hickey. Marking me as *his*.

I pull his face to meet mine and kiss him deeply, an *I want to fuck you* kiss that he must feel all the way to the tips of his toes. He shudders slightly, pulling me towards him, and I feel his

SEVEN SONS

hardness against the itch of my fresh ink and tentatively covered scars.

"Do you have to leave?" I ask sweetly, after we break apart. "We only just started having fun."

"Ugh!" Dornan groans. "You're killing me, princess. I gotta run. The boys are waiting for me. I'll see you in a day or two."

I nod, trying to appear sad, and I yelp as he slaps my ass again.

"Watch her," he says, stabbing Jase's chest with his finger. "I'm out."

He leaves without looking back, and I relax immediately.

"Happy that he's gone?" Jase asks darkly.

I had forgotten that he was there for a moment. Christ. I really need to keep my wits about me.

"I'm hungry," I explain. "All the man wants to do is fuck, and I haven't eaten since lunchtime yesterday."

He gives me a look so withering, it takes all of my will not to break down and tell him who I really am. I didn't anticipate having to be in the same room as him, let alone be babysat by him. Being judged like a common whore by him.

Jase strides over to the open window that separates the kitchen from the dining room. "Hey, Carol, you there?" he asks, in a voice more like a teddy bear's than the asshole tone he's been using with me.

Before I can think, a woman pops her head around the corner of the kitchen doorway, smiling.

"Hey, Jase," she says, ruffling his hair. I swallow hard and look for an escape that doesn't exist.

"Sammi here missed breakfast. Do you think we could grab some cereal or something from the pantry?"

Carol wipes her hands on a dishrag and smiles, looking straight at me. I freeze like a deer in headlights.

She is only forty but looks closer to fifty, a life of excess and violence written in each deep line that draws out from underneath

49

her huge green eyes. Her dark blonde hair sits atop her head in a messy French bun, peppered with fine slivers of grey.

"Hello, Sammi," Carol says, extending her hand. "You must be new here. I can fix you anything – eggs? Toast?"

"Cereal is fine," I squeak as I shake my mother's hand.

TEN

MY MOTHER SOLD ME OUT for a bag of blow.

There.

I said it.

She was a terrible mother, a liar and a whore and a thief. Falling pregnant with me was an accident – she was barely seventeen and had just met my father.

Growing up, my father was like a mother to me as well. And my mother, when she was around, was like a distant older sister who lashed out at me when I did something wrong, and yelled at me whenever I cried. I learned from a very early age never to cry. I perfected my poker face at three years old, the same age I learned how to climb out of my own cot, how to pull up a chair and fix myself breakfast, and how to call 911 when my mother overdosed on heroin in the bath.

She was a horrid mother, but she was still my mother, and I loved her more than anything.

The day Dornan took me – the day I "died" – was like any other day. My father was still at work at the factory; my mother was tearing at her skin, out of cash and out of meth.

Then Uncle Dornan knocked at the door, flanked by Chad and Maxi. I was a streetwise kid. I'd grown up in the life, in the club. I could see the guns bulging at their waistbands, concealed under thin shirts and patched leather jackets.

My mother answered the door. I was in the kitchen, and heard voices. They were looking for my father, was he home?

When my mother told him that my father was still at work, Dornan burst in, apparently unsatisfied with her answer.

Then his eyes landed on me, and a shit-eating grin grew on his beard-stubbled face.

"You'd better come with us, Juliette," he said, his voice like sharp gravel scraping against my bare skin.

I looked at my mother, alarmed. Something wasn't right.

"Why?" my mother asked, picking at her arm like she did when she was hanging for a fix.

Dornan withdrew a knotted baggie of light brown powder from inside his jacket and held it in front of her. Heroin.

"Relax, darlin'," he said, grinning. I felt my skin prickle as my heart thudded faster. "We'll have you back here in a few hours."

My mother looked uncertain. "Why do you need Julie?" she asked. She always called me Julie. Everyone else called me Julz.

Except Dornan. He liked to use my full name.

Dornan shook the baggie. "We just need her to help us find something, Carol. It's a quick in-and-out job. Nothing untoward."

My mother bit her lip and looked from Dornan, to me, to the baggie.

"I don't feel well," I said to my mother, backing away. "I don't want to go."

Dornan stepped closer to me, towering over my five-feet-tall frame. "It's important, Juliette," he said, his smile vanishing. "Jason's waiting for you."

He grabbed my elbow, steering me towards the front door.

"Mom," I protested.

Dornan dropped the bag into her open palm and smiled victoriously. "You're a good woman, Carol. I knew you'd help us."

"Have her home for dinner," my mother said, turning and fleeing to the kitchen with her drugs.

Dornan tugged me more forcefully. "Mom!" I yelled. She didn't answer. She ignored my pleading as three men dragged me out of my house and ordered me into the backseat of their car, the engine still running.

"Where are we going?" I asked them, annoyed and upset.

Nobody answered. Dornan didn't make eye contact with me, just glanced up and down our street before slamming my door shut. A moment later, he was in the driver's seat, and activated the central locking. I was trapped.

I rested my head against my window and stared at my house for what would be the last time.

I watched my mother through the open curtains as Dornan reversed the car out of our driveway. She looked completely engrossed as she drew up cloudy liquid into a syringe.

She didn't even look up from fixing her hit as her only daughter was driven to her death.

I SIT IN STUNNED SILENCE, shovelling Cheerios into my mouth, thankful that as the grains melt on my tongue, they are washing away the taste of Dornan's parting kiss.

I am faltering.

I don't know if I can do this.

Not now that I have seen my own mother stare through me as if I were a complete stranger.

She thinks I'm dead. I am experiencing a type of mourning for her, one that I never expected to feel. She is a traitor, after all. I think she knew what Dornan was planning to do to my father, but she didn't care. She didn't leave, or warn my father or me. No, instead she ran to Dornan, begging for money for her meth habit, *always begging for money*, and even when I supposedly died at his hands, she still didn't leave this godforsaken place.

"You look like you've seen a ghost," Jase says quietly, swinging back on his chair so that only the rear two legs are touching the ground.

I drop my spoon into my milky bowl and wipe my mouth with the back of my hand.

"Am I going to get a running commentary the entire time your father is gone?" I ask, pushing my bowl away. "Because I'd rather not."

He seems surprised at my sudden turn in mood, and, to be honest, so am I. I thought screwing Dornan and having him stare at me like a sick puppy was going to be the most difficult part of this whole thing.

Clearly, I was wrong.

Jase widens his eyes and smiles cheekily. "Hello. Is this the real Samantha? Because I like her more than the fairy floss bullshit you spin in front of Dornan."

I smile back, but my smile is sour. "Look," I breathe, leaning over the table, "I like your father, don't get me wrong. He's given me a place to stay and money to sort myself out. But—"

"What?" Jase teases, swinging dangerously far back on the chair before slamming the front two legs back onto the ground so that his face is closer to mine. "You don't like being cooped up inside while Pop goes off with his merry band?"

I drop the smile. "Something like that."

Jase sniffs and nods, scanning the room. "I get it. This isn't what you signed up for."

"Exactly," I say. "I'm grateful, don't get me wrong. I'm just a little ... *overwhelmed* right now."

Jase narrows his eyes, seemingly in deep thought. "Be careful around here," he says. "Things – people – have a way of getting hurt if they don't do what they're told."

Please Pop, please don't, they're hurting her, please stop, STOP STOP STOP.

I just nod, chewing on my lip. "Thanks for the tip."

"So, you hate storms?" Jase says, cocking his head to the side.

He is still trying to figure me out, I think. He still suspects I'm more than just a fuck buddy of his father's.

"I hate humidity," I shrug. "That's all."

"Huh." He is silent for a moment, then stands abruptly. "You wanna come up to the roof for a while?"

Isn't that where the fucking storm is?

"I mean, unless you're scared." It's an open challenge that he extends to me with an outstretched palm and a cocky grin. Asshole.

I smile, putting my hand in his and standing up. "Only if you straighten my hair afterwards," I say playfully.

"Ahhh... deal? I guess? How the hell do you straighten your hair anyway?"

"With a flatiron," I smile. "Game?"

"I guess," he says, not looking too convinced. As he leads me back to the hallway, he reaches his free arm around the doorway and snipes a bottle of Jack from the kitchen.

"For the light show," he winks, waving the bottle.

I just smile a lie as my stomach flips and my heart sinks all in one.

ELEVEN

THE CLUBHOUSE HAS FEW WINDOWS and a lot of soundproofing, a dream for a girl who is terrified of thunder and lightning.

The minute we get to the top of the stairwell and Jase opens the fire escape, I am cringing at the bright flashes of light and the menacing thunder that rips through every fiber of my being.

Once the door is open, the noise of the wind and thunder becomes deafening, and I cower at the prospect of going out into it.

"Come on," Jase yells above the din, pulling my hand. "Trust me!"

Trust him? Of course *I* trust him. He risked his goddamn life to try and save mine all those years ago.

But does *Sammi* trust him? *Should she?*

"Fuck it," I breathe, unplanting my stubborn feet and following him outside into the howling wind and neon flashes. It's got to be better that being stuck downstairs with my *mother*.

I squint my eyes, cringing against the sudden assault of stinging, sharp raindrops that are almost solid enough to be considered hail. They bite at my skin like tiny bullets, baying for my blood.

"Why the hell do you want to be out here?" I yell at Jase. He tugs my hand and we keep running. The visibility is terrible and I can barely see what's in front of me, apart from thick sheets of icy rain.

Lightning strikes uncomfortably close and I scream, practically jumping on Jase. He laughs, pointing at something in front of us. At first, I don't realize what it is – it's a room without walls, and it's not wet inside.

It's not magic, it's a room made entirely of glass. A greenhouse.

How odd, I think, and squeal again when another bolt of lightning strikes less than a hundred feet away. I am practically glued to Jase like a spider monkey stuck to his back.

I breathe a sigh of relief as he opens a door in the glass and pulls me inside, closing it behind us. The storm still rages around us, but at least I feel a little more protected. The room is pretty big, at least twenty feet across and with a stunning view of the Venice Beach coastline.

"What is this place?" I ask. "A marijuana farm?"

Jase smiles. "Used to be. Until the cops started doing aerial surveillance. Now it's my hangout when I get sick of being down there with my idiot brothers."

"Do you bring all your father's whores up here?" I ask him, wringing the extra moisture out of my long brown hair.

Jase chuckles. "Did you just call yourself a whore?"

I smile wickedly. "Let's keep ourselves firmly planted in reality, shall we? I'm sleeping with your father so he'll let me stay here in his club. What else would you call me?"

Jase raises his eyebrows. "I don't know. A girl who had to make some hard decisions to protect herself?"

I shrug, shivering. "That's a much nicer way of saying it," I concede.

"Here." Jase shrugs out of his long-sleeved leather jacket and puts it around my shoulders. I can't help but notice that the jacket

is plain, devoid of any patches or club insignia. That must piss
Dornan right off.

"Thanks," I say, a thrill coursing through me as his fingertips
brush my shoulder.

I am amazed. Even after six years, even with him oblivious to
who I actually am, there is a chemistry between us that cracks and
fizzes like the storm that rages all around us.

"Take a seat," Jase says, pulling out a couple of upended milk
crates. He sits on one and produces a half-empty bag of pretzels
to go with the bottle of Jack at his feet. He munches on a pretzel
before offering me the bag.

I take it, eating a pretzel and watching as he unscrews the
whiskey and takes a long, deep drink. I imagine how it must burn
his throat, his tongue, his lips.

His lips.

"Do you always start drinking at ten in the morning?" I ask
him.

He grins cheekily and looks at me from underneath his thick
black eyelashes. He has his mother's dimpled smile, and for that I
am eternally grateful.

"Only when I'm babysitting *whores*," he jokes, offering me the
bottle. I take a swig and the liquid burns all the way down to my
stomach.

"You don't even know me," I say, popping another pretzel in
my mouth. "I don't even think you *like* me. Why bother bringing
me up here?"

Jase takes the bottle back and takes a swig, gulping the
burning liquid down. He studies me for a moment, giving me an
uneasy feeling in my belly.

Because he looks at me like he *does* know me.

"You remind me of a girl I used to know," he says quietly,
looking away.

"Oh, really?" I ask casually, a river of pent-up tears burning a
hole in my fucking heart. "Where is she now?"

He looks at the ground for a moment before meeting my gaze again. "She died."

I swallow back the enormous lump in my throat. I can't cry. If I cry, this is all over. And it can't be over, not yet.

"I'm sorry," I say quietly, my carefully laid plans threatening to shatter to pieces like the flimsy glass building we are sheltered within.

"It's fine," he says, waving his hand dismissively. "It was a long time ago."

We sit there in silence for awhile, munching on pretzels and sharing the Jack. After awhile I start to feel relaxed.

Stop drinking. You need to keep your wits about you.

"Your dad's a little... full on," I say finally, piercing the silence.

Jase looks at me with an expression devoid of laughter or light. "He's one of a kind," he says, and I can hear the bitterness in his voice.

"You two aren't close?" *Please say no, please say no.*

"Huh!" Jase chuckles, but there is no joy in the sound. It is more like a strangled cry of desperation.

"No. We're not close." There is so much more behind those words, a story I can tell he wants to share, but he's smart not to. He doesn't know me. I could go and blab everything he's telling me to Dornan.

"He's kind of scary, isn't he?" I say gingerly, not sure how much he'll reveal.

He just stares at me with his watery blue eyes until I want to blush under the power of his gaze. "What?" I say. "Did I say too much? I'm sorry." I shift uncomfortably as he continues to watch me.

"You're kind of freaking me out," I say finally, looking away.

"Sorry," he says, the tension broken. "I just–"

"You just what?"

He leans closer to me and looks around nervously. "You need to be careful," he says, the worry in his voice clear. "You seem like a nice girl. My father meets girls like you and gets a little obsessed."

"I've noticed," I say, no humor left in my voice now either. I shake my head. "I just wanted a job," I whisper. "Now he's got me here, I feel like he won't let me leave."

"He won't," Jason says flatly. "My father's fucking intense. He wants you, he'll have you."

I look at him, horrified. I remember Dornan being obsessive and calculating when I was a child, but not like this.

Although, he did organize for his sons to take turns raping a fifteen year old girl who called him Uncle. So, its not terribly surprising, I suppose.

"You'll be fine," he says quickly, seeing my face. "Just don't piss him off. He'll get a new obsession in a month or two, and then you can breathe easy."

I nod, suddenly overwhelmed and claustrophobic despite being in a room with see-through walls. I take the bottle from Jase and have a long, deep drink from it. Screw staying sober. I don't know how the fuck I'm going to deal with being Dornan's prisoner when all I came here for was to dance at the burlesque club and get close to the clubhouse. *This close* wasn't part of the plan. Although, at the same time, it's deliciously convenient and will no doubt speed things up considerably.

"What happened to his last obsession?"

Jase takes the bottle back but doesn't drink. He is thinking.

"Maybe I don't want to know," I say reluctantly.

"I can't talk about it," Jase says finally. "I just met you. He's my father."

I nod, but inside I'm deflated. Jase is *protecting* him. He's protecting Dornan, who held his high school sweetheart down and raped her. While he made Jase watch.

"I get it," I say flatly. "He's your father. Of course you want to be loyal to him."

Jase appears pained. "Want to? *Have* to. You think you're the only one trapped here with no way out?"

I swallow thickly and sit there, my heart pounding in my chest.

Not protecting him.

Being held hostage by him.

It all makes perfect sense now.

WE STAY IN THE GLASS house for hours, eventually talking of lighter things, only leaving when the sun decides to slip below the horizon. By the time we do, something has definitely shifted between Jase and Sammi. Which is a wonderful thing to cling to amongst the madness I am drowning in.

When I finally collapse into Dornan's king-sized bed at midnight, tipsy and exhausted, I can only hope that he stays away another day.

TWELVE

WHEN I WAKE IN THE morning, I am still alone. Thank Christ for small miracles. After spending a blessed day with Jase, the last thing I want to do is wake up to a nightmare. I have a pit in the bottom of my stomach when I wake up, a nervous, cloying tension that something is wrong. I wonder if it's because Elliot is going crazy trying to contact my useless, smashed phone.

There is a soft knock at the door and I sit up, tensed for whoever might be there, and wishing I had a gun. I relax when Jase sticks his head in.

"Awake?"

"Yeah," I reply, stretching lazily. I stand up, brightening when I see he is holding a tray with two coffee cups.

"My father's on his way back," he says. "Should be here any minute. You want breakfast?" He holds up a brown paper bag. "I grabbed bagels."

I love bagels. "Sure," I say. "Just let me get changed."

"Meet you on the roof," he says, leaving my coffee on the dresser next to the door.

I sip the coffee as I change into a sleeveless turquoise-colored dress with little lace details cut into the hem. I had to buy a whole new wardrobe when I had my boobs done. Nothing from my old life fits me anymore, which is kind of a good thing. New clothes for a new identity.

I slip my feet into clear plastic flip flops and tie my hair in a messy bun on top of my head. Grabbing my sunglasses and my coffee, I head up to the roof.

This morning, the storm has cleared and the view of the ocean is stunning. Jase has buttered two blueberry bagels and sat them on a brown paper bag on the edge of the building, which comes up to my waist.

"Thanks for breakfast," I say, shoving a piece of buttery bagel in my mouth and following it with a slug of warm latte. "I would've settled for Cheerios and instant coffee, but this is delicious."

Jase smiles. "No problem. The first one's free."

"Oh, really?" I ask. "What does the next one cost?"

He opens his mouth to answer me, but before he does, the fire escape door bursts open and several of the Ross brothers appear. I almost choke on the bagel in my throat.

"They're up here!" Chad calls down the stairs.

I stand there, looking for a weapon just in case. I don't know what they're up to. I don't trust any of them for a second.

Except Jase.

My worst nightmare arrives at the top of the stairs, bound, gagged, and bloody.

Fuck.

Dornan pushes the poor boy forward, and I rush to them, freaking the fuck out.

This is bad. This is so very, very bad.

"Baby girl!" Dornan booms, clearly amped up on a mixture of adrenalin and some kind of drug, probably crystal meth. "Got you a gift!"

"Dornan," I stutter. "What are you doing?"

Dornan removes the boy's gag, and grabs the back of his neck, pointing his gaze towards me.

"Remember her, motherfucker?!" Dornan demands, spittle flying from his mouth and landing on the boy's face.

"Dornan, it's not what you think!"

"Shut your mouth," Dornan yells at me. "Let him speak."

Oh God. What am I going to do?

"Dornan, he's not who you think he is–"

"Chad, shut her the fuck *up*, will you?" Dornan points to me and before I can move, Chad has sidled up alongside me and grabbed me in a bear hug, his hand planted firmly over my mouth. I gasp, unable to scream. I look over at Jase, whose peaceful breakfast has been shattered by all the ruckus.

"Pop," Jase says slowly, "what's going on? Who the hell is this guy?"

"What's your name, son?" Dornan demands. "Speak!"

"M-Michael."

Michael Trevine.

I just have one question for you, baby girl.

The boy is terrified. One of his eyes is swollen shut, there is blood all over him, and I wonder how much of the long journey back to LA was spent beating him.

Tears form at the corner of my eyes as the full brunt of Dornan's obsession with me becomes apparent. He left me here for *this*. He asked me who my ex-boyfriend was, and then proceeded to travel across the country to kidnap an innocent boy from his house. A boy who has never laid eyes on me, a boy who I found online and added to Sammi's backstory for credibility.

A boy with a gun pointed at his head.

I struggle against Chad's stronghold, but it is useless. The guy is built, and he's probably been snorting the white powder with Daddy Dornan all the way home.

I bite down on Chad's hand and he pulls it away, yelling at me.

"He's not my ex!" I scream, fighting against Chad's rigid embrace.

Dornan looks at me like a man possessed. A man on a mission.

"I lied," I gasp, still struggling. "I've never met him before. Please, just let him go."

Dornan lowers his gun and looks me up and down. "You don't have to be scared of him anymore," he says.

He lifts the gun, his finger putting pressure on the trigger.

"Please!" I scream.

My pleas go unheeded.

He pulls the trigger.

Two things happen. Firstly, the roar of a single bullet as it leaves Dornan's gun and enters the back of the boy's head. Secondly, almost at the exact same time, I am showered with a fine mist of blood and what I think are pieces of Michael Trevine's skull.

Michael lays on the ground, motionless. The red cloud around his head grows swiftly, reaching my flip flops. I scream and Chad releases me, letting me slump to the ground. I crawl through blood and bits of skull to get to the dead boy, cradling him in my arms. He is heavy, a dead weight, because he is dead. And it is my fault.

I heft the boy onto my lap and realize his eyes are still open.

Fuck.

With trembling fingers, I reach over and press his eyelids shut.

I feel hands on my shoulders, pulling me away, and it takes everything inside me not to kick and claw and bite Dornan as he carries me away. He pulls my clothes off and puts me in the shower, where I huddle into a ball and stare at the lines of grout that separate each white tile.

You don't have to be scared of him anymore.

I make a strangled sobbing sound, but nothing much comes out of my throat except a dried-up, pathetic scream.

Dornan pulls me from the shower, wraps me in a towel and walks me to his bed, where he sits me down.

"Do you understand how much I care about you now?" Dornan asks with a throat full of gravel. His hands are all over me, feverish, and I don't fight back when he presses me down onto the bed and unbuckles his belt.

I just lay there, in shock, his lips at my throat and his hands roving every inch of my shell-shocked body.

"Do you know why I did that?" he breathes in my ear as he grips my hips and slides inside me.

My breath hitches in my throat as he begins to thrust into me, and I feel a single tear roll down the side of my face.

"Because I'm yours," I whisper into the darkness.

THIRTEEN

IF I THINK WATCHING MICHAEL die in front of me for a careless lie I created is bad, the aftermath is horrific.

Dornan is high, the blood on his hands washed clean away but still leaving invisible handprints all over my body that spell *murderer.*

Because it is my fault. I should never have used a real person's name in my fake past; I should have just made one up.

It seems that the only thing that gets Dornan hornier than a girl auditioning for a job by screwing him is killing her supposed ex-boyfriend. The hours after he shoots Michael are possibly even worse than the night six years ago when Dornan and his sons took turns raping me. Because at least then I could struggle.

At least then I could scream.

Now, here, it is like I am in a hell that I will never escape. Six years' worth of nightmares are coming to life in the space of a few incredibly torturous hours.

Dornan is high and he wants to fuck.

"What's wrong, baby girl?" he keeps asking me over and over as I lay flat on my back, being fucked, unable to move.

I just have one question, baby girl.

After it has been going on for an hour or maybe more, I clear my raw throat.

"Stop," I plead.

He doesn't stop.

I push his warm chest away from mine. I can't breathe. I threw up my breakfast in the shower as I watched Michael's blood and pieces of skull rinse from my skin and drift lazily down the drain, gone forever. I am shaky and starving.

For a moment, I think he will stop, afford me a small rest before he starts up again.

"Please?" I ask him. "Please just stop for a minute."

He doesn't stop.

It's the drugs, I realize. He is frustrated. He is hard and he is horny and the drugs are stopping him from having that release that he needs so desperately to calm down.

"Stop!" I yell, pushing his chest with all my might. Surprisingly, he doesn't pin me down as I suspected he would, but draws himself out of me and rolls to the side, coming to a standing position beside the bed. I draw my knees up to my chest and watch in horror as he pulls a shiny black gun from his side table.

It is only now that I see his entire body is shaking, balanced precariously on the edge of an overdose.

"What did you take?" I ask calmly, sitting up on the side of the bed. I am alarmed. He can't die, not now, not before he suffers for me. It would be too easy for him to just OD and die before I've made him regret ever meeting my father.

He doesn't answer, just starts to pace the room, his cock still erect in front of him, his index finger nervously bouncing against the trigger of his gun.

"Dornan, you need to calm down," I say, still in shock and not ready for him to shoot me, too. "You've taken something."

"Too pure," he says, "too pure. We gotta cut it down, cut it down—"

"Hey!" I say loudly, trying to cut through his incoherent monologue.

He swings around and presses the tip of the gun to my forehead. I gasp.

"Why did you come here?" he asks me, his breathing short and sharp. He is angry. Angry and peaking.

Stick to the story.

"I had nowhere else to go," I say honestly, and it is true. *I had nowhere else to go.*

"You know what I did for you? The risk I took?" I nod.

"I know. Thank you for protecting me." The words are pouring out of my mouth before I can even think. I will do anything for him to take the gun away from my head and calm down.

"I fucking risked EVERYTHING for you, and you don't even care?"

Oh God. *Oh Godohgodohgod.*

"I do care," I say, and I do the only thing I can think to do to calm him down. I take his cock in my hands and start stroking back and forth, making a tight fist. He seems to relax almost immediately, but doesn't take the gun away. I look up at him through my eyelashes and see his face still incredibly tense, his body twitching with too much pent-up energy and high-grade methamphetamine.

I have to do something. I take his cock and guide it gently to my mouth, teasing the underside with the tip of my tongue. His whole body is still shaking but he moans and drops the gun to his side, his other hand stroking my hair.

I keep going, thankful that I at least don't have to look at him. I pretend that we are other people, somewhere else, and this, too, makes it easier to keep going. I sigh with relief when the gun clatters to the floor and he uses both hands to grip the sides of my head.

"Baby girl," he moans, rocking his hips in rhythm, his cock as hard as ever.

I take him all in, as far as my mouth will open, and he suddenly tenses. "Ohhhh," I hear him say as hot cum hits the back of my throat. It takes every muscle in my body locked rigid so that I don't choke. I am suddenly overwhelmed by a claustrophobic, trapped sensation that goes from my mouth all the way down to my stomach.

Dornan staggers back, a sated smile on his handsome face. I swallow thickly, looking around the room for something – anything – to get the taste of him out of my mouth. I spy my half-drunk coffee from the morning, sitting innocently on the nightstand. I have no idea how it got here. I reach for it and take a swig of the cold liquid, sighing as it floods my mouth with sugar and bitterness. My eye notices something on the cup and I look closer.

I shudder.

A fine mist of blood coats the Styrofoam, and I drop the cup to the floor as if it has burned me.

I turn my hand over to see that some of the blood is flecked on my palm. Disgusted, I wipe my hand on the dark bed sheets. I look up to see Dornan has already passed out face-down on the bed in the space of about ten seconds.

I finish wiping my hand and fish a pair of skinny jeans and an oversized black t-shirt printed with a skull and crossbones out of my suitcase at the end of the bed. I dress quickly and tiptoe out of the room as quietly as I can. Making my way to the roof, I take the stairs two at a time. I need fresh air in my lungs or I will scream.

Pushing the fire escape door open, I am panting audibly. I am two steps outside when I realize my error in choosing to visit Michael's place of execution. I try to back up when I discover I've forgotten to wedge the fire escape open. *Fuck.* I am stuck out here, with the afternoon sun beating down on my skull, blood at my feet. *At least they took the body away.*

I can't look at the floor or I will throw up, and I've got nothing left in my stomach. The concrete is still damp with someone's efforts to hose the blood away, and I cringe as I think of the poor boy's blood now coating the entire roof floor in microscopic detail. I focus on the sea breeze ahead of me, the glare of the afternoon sun overhead, the ocean lapping lazily at the shore a few blocks ahead. I am so preoccupied with the view, leaning against the waist-high wall with my palms digging into sharp brick edges, that I almost fall off the side of the building as I hear a crash behind me.

I startle, turning to see where the noise has come from. It is Jase. He looks worried. When I see him, I almost cry. But I don't. I swallow back bitter tears and turn back to the view of Venice Beach, unable or unwilling to look at him – I'm not sure which.

I feel him take up a spot beside be and flinch when he passes something in front of my face.

"Hey," he says, steadying me with the slightest touch of his palm on my shoulder. "I cleaned your sunglasses. Don't fall off the roof, okay?"

I take the sunglasses and put them on, relieved that the throbbing sun is now a little less intense.

"Where did you go?" he asks.

I press my fingers into the sharp bricks, to keep myself from breaking down.

"With your father," I bite out.

Now I am the one shaking. My skin is slick with sweat and heat radiates from me, but I am so cold, my teeth are chattering.

"Hey," Jase says, and I can hear the worry in his voice. "Come on." He presses his hand in the small of my back, as if to lead me away from the edge, and I flinch, backing away from his hand. He holds his palms up in a supplicating gesture and shrugs.

"I was just going to get you a seat, that's all," he says. "You hungry? I can get you some food."

Food. My stomach decides for me. I follow him blindly towards the greenhouse, stumbling in bare feet and too-long jeans, tiptoeing around the wettest part of the concrete – the place where Michael Trevine bled out.

"Here." He points to a worn, brown leather chair that wasn't there yesterday. "Sit here. I'll grab you something to eat. I can hear your frigging stomach growling from here."

I sink into the chair, thankful for the weight off my legs. I grip the leather armrests and time passes, how much I'm not sure. The only point of reference I have is the sun, which has moved from overhead to in front of me. I estimate that it's about five in the afternoon when a thought suddenly slams into my brain like a freight train.

Elliot.

Shit. I need to call him. I need to go to him. Right fucking *now.* The urge to flee this place has me itching all over. I want to get out. I want to get out. *Iwanttogetout.*

Jase returns after a while, balancing a plate of what looks like some kind of meat casserole with mashed potato. It smells like my childhood.

Fuck. I can't do this.

"Carol was serving dinner to the boys," he says, handing me the plate and a fork. I take the plate, my hunger beating the emotions I feel at the prospect of my mother cooking this meal for the Ross brothers a few rooms away while I was giving my father's murderer a blow job. I demolish the plate in record time and briefly consider licking it clean. If I were alone, I definitely would.

I set the plate down at my feet and stare ahead blankly.

"Are you okay?" Jase asks me, his voice tinged with fear.

"No," I reply.

"I told you, my dad can get pretty obsessed sometimes. Just ... be careful what you say to him, okay?"

I nod vacantly, chewing on my lip.

"I'm sorry for what happened. Really. My brothers are just like him. They're animals sometimes."

I know that.

"Is there anything I can … do for you? Get for you?"

I don't answer him.

"Samantha?"

I tear my gaze from the floor to meet his pinched eyes. "I want to get out of here," I say to him. "Just for a few hours. Just to cool off. Do you think you can help me with that?"

I have to get to Elliot before he comes looking for me here. They will kill him if he turns up, I am sure of it.

Jase nods, seemingly relieved that I have broken out of my stupor to respond to him.

"Yeah," he says, patting my closed fist with his hand. "Let's get out of here."

When I don't move, he waves his hand in front of my face. "Earth to Samantha?"

The gentle way he says *Samantha* makes my heart leap a little.

"How come you don't call me Sammi?" I ask him as he offers his hand and pulls me up to my feet.

He furrows his eyebrows. "I don't know. Samantha is classy. It suits you better."

"Classy," I repeat. "Pfft. I don't know where you got that idea from."

He looks at me with a serious look on his face, still frowning. "What?" I say.

He shrugs. "You don't really belong here, in a place like this. I thought that from the minute I saw you."

You have no idea how wrong you are.

"I grew up in a place just like this," I reply. "It's just like home."

He doesn't answer me, but his eyes are full of questions. Full of worry. Full of the past.

"Come on," I say. "Let's get out of here before your father wakes up."

73

FOURTEEN

I FOLLOW JASE DOWN THE stairs and through the kitchen. I don't look into the servery – the last thing I want to see is my mother when I'm leaving, and I don't know if I'm coming back.

I am scared.

I forgot how crazy Dornan Ross was.

And I can't get the image of that poor kid's blood and brain matter out of my mind.

When Jase turns left at the hallway, I hesitate.

"Come on," he says. "My bike's this way."

"Oh," I say. "I thought we'd just go in a car or something."

He smirks and looks me up and down. "We're in a biker club, *Samantha*, not a goddamn minivan club."

"I don't have a helmet. Or a jacket." I look down at my bare feet. "Or shoes."

Jase just laughs as he continues down the hallway. "You think you're the first girl who ever came in without a helmet, jacket, or shoes?"

Well, I don't have anything to say to that. I just shrug in response.

Jase slides the thick steel door at the end of the hallway open, and ushers me inside. I immediately smell oil, leather, and sweat

74

all mingled together. I look around, taking in the impressive line-up of Harley Davidsons that sit two and three deep in the massive garage.

"That's a lot of bikes," I breathe, squinting under the harsh fluorescent lights that illuminate the warehouse-sized space.

Jase goes over to the far wall and rummages through a clear tub full of helmets. Fishing one out, he gestures for me to come over. I thread my way carefully through the maze of metal, mindful that if I knock one bike, I'll start a domino effect of epic proportions.

He puts the helmet on the counter next to him and hands me a pair of women's white canvas sneakers. They are at least a size too big for me, but I bend down to lace them tightly so they will stay on my feet.

Next, he grabs a beaten, chocolate-colored leather jacket from a hook above the counter and passes it to me. I shrug into it and find the zip, pulling it up to my chin.

"Here," he says, fitting the open-face helmet on my head. "How's this?"

I am about to reply, but the door is dragged open again and loud voices fill the once-peaceful space.

It is two of the Ross brothers – Chad, who held his hand over my mouth as I screamed for Dornan to spare an innocent life, and Mickey, the fourth brother.

They are chatting in an animated fashion, every second word *Fuck*, when they lay eyes on me.

"Hey, darlin'," Chad says, striding through the silent motorcycles to where we stand. "Where you off to?"

Jase looks at him without a single ounce of brotherly affection. "I'm taking her for a ride, Chad," he bites out. "Nothing for you to worry about."

Chad slides between his brother and I, forcing Jase to step back. His chest is pressed into mine but I stand my ground, looking up at him through a haze of violent memories, my jaw set stubbornly.

"Sorry about your little boyfriend," he says with a broad smile, not sorry at all. He runs a finger down my arm, from shoulder to wrist, and smirks when I jerk my hand away.

"Sorry about your little hand," I reply, not taking my eyes off him for a second.

His smile twitches, and for a moment I get the oddest sensation that he is going to take a swing at me. Instead, he leans real close, so that I can feel his breath on my face. It smells sickly sweet, like pineapple flavoring or those ultra-caffeinated energy drinks.

"I know what you're up to," he says menacingly. "You think you can just come in here because you're screwing my pop? It ain't that simple, sugar. There are rules around here."

I raise my eyebrows and laugh, unnerving him. "Your father's head over heels for me. I doubt very much anything you have to say will sway his mind."

The smirk reappears on his face, and he slams me against the wall with brute force, planting his hands on either side of me so that I am effectively trapped.

"Hey!" Jase bellows, trying to pull his hulkish brother away from me.

Mickey suddenly appears and pulls Jase roughly by the back of his shirt. "He's not going to hurt her, brother," he says. He seems irritated, and bored. Everyone here is always either cruel or bored.

"Yeah," Chad drawls, grinding himself against me. The move isn't sexual so much as dominating. "I'm not gonna hurt her, baby brother." With that, he yanks my black t-shirt up with one hand and rips the clear plastic dressing off my stomach with the other.

Fuck.

The lighting is so bright in here, and the coloring isn't finished. Can he see my scars?

He scrapes his calloused hand along the length of my freshly scabbed tattoo, making me wince. He studies the design, poking and prodding, before letting my t-shirt fall again, apparently satisfied.

"Nice tatt," he says, baring his teeth in a vicious smile.

"Thanks," I spit back. "If you wanted to see it, all you had to do was ask."

"I don't ask, sugar. I tell. And you know what else I've got to tell you?"

I roll my eyes. "I'm sure you're about to give it to me."

He leans close and whispers in my ear. "When you get angry, you lose that little southern drawl you're putting on, sweetheart."

I don't visibly react, because I already know he is suspicious of me, but inside I turn cold and fill with dread.

"That Michael boy hadn't seen your slut face in his lifetime," he spits. "I'm onto you, darlin'. And once I figure out what you're playing at, it's game over for you."

I don't answer. Any argument I put forward is going to sound like defensiveness. I think of ten different comebacks, and every one of them makes me look culpable.

"You're crazy," I say instead.

He grins and steps back, still observing me closely. "Crazy smart," he replies. His eyes look funny, and I'm guessing that he is just as high as Dornan was when he was insatiable this morning.

"That's enough," Jase says, pushing his brother aside. This time, Chad lets him, laughing.

"You like her, baby brother?" he teases. "You wanna fuck her? Because Pop doesn't share his women with his sons."

Jase ignores him, handing me my helmet and guiding me by my hand to his motorbike, which sits in a sea of identical bikes.

"Check her for weapons!" Chad calls to his brother, laughing like an asshole. "Cavity search the bitch in case she has a knife hiding up there in her lying pussy."

I turn my head to glare at him and he grins. I remember that grin. It is the grin of a thousand nightmares. The grin of someone without a soul. The grin of a firstborn son who has been given a virgin to rape as penance for her father's sins.

As the oldest brother, Chad had been given the green light to go first. His younger brothers pinned me down, one on each hand and another holding my feet.

Chad's eyes lit up like a kid on Christmas morning when he approached me, his jeans unzipped and his erection full and tight in his hand.

"You sure you don't want to do this, Pop?" he asked Dornan, his eyes full of lust and malevolence.

Dornan laughed and shook his head, slapping his oldest son on the back. My eyes grew wide as he lowered himself onto me and forced his leg between my thighs, creating a juncture.

I did the only thing I could think to do. I started to beg. "Please don't do this," I begged him. "Chad, please. I've never ... I've never done it before." Shame at being exposed in front of eight men turned my skin red and I began to cry again.

Chad grinned that grin, and I started to struggle against the hands that held me down. I bucked and screamed like a wild animal caught in a snare as Chad draped himself over me, a wicked glint in his eyes. I squeezed my eyes shut, unwilling to see what I knew he was-about to do.

And then. Pain. Burning, searing pain that never stopped. It felt like I would break in half. I screamed so loud, my throat felt like it would collapse. A hand covered my mouth, muffling my sounds, and I bit down on that soft flesh, choking as I tasted coppery blood spring forth.

"Bitch!" Chad yelled, punching me in the jaw so hard I felt bone crack. I gargled an unintelligible noise as something soft, some kind of fabric, was stuffed into my mouth to still my screams.

"Well, I'll be goddamned," Chad groaned, as I burned and cried. "Tight little bitch was telling the truth."

I tear my gaze away from Chad, a scowl on my face, and watch impatiently as Jase kicks his bike over. It roars to life, the sweet sound of a roaring Harley and the exhaust fumes conjuring a lifetime of happier memories of my father. I focus on those, trying desperately not to slip back into that other memory, determined not to let Chad best me before I've even put up a fight. Jase nods his head to the side and I swing my leg over the seat of the bike, shuffling forward and wrapping my arms around his hard midsection.

The minute my feet are securely braced on the passenger pegs, Jase takes off, and I hold on tighter as he accelerates. He maneuvers the beast of a bike deftly through the stack of other gleaming machines, until we are at the roller door. He fishes a remote out of his pocket and presses a button on it, sending the roller door skywards. Sunlight drowns the artificial light and I squint without my sunglasses.

My entire body relaxes as we leave the confines of the clubhouse and drive through the open gate, the bike hugging the road as Jase rides with precision and skill. I can feel a smile growing wider on my face as my long hair whips behind me, my legs snugly wrapped around the first boy I ever loved. Even if he doesn't know who I am, even if he can never know... in this moment, just to be alone with him, on the open road, is enough for me.

After we get a few miles, Jase slows the bike and pulls over to the shoulder. Smiling, he turns his head and speaks. "Where to?" he asks. *Elliot.*

"I need to get this tattoo colored in," I say, loud enough so that he can hear me over the roar of the engine. "Lost City Tattoos?"

He nods and turns back to the road, checks his mirrors, and we take off again, destined for Elliot and his needles and his questions.

I think I need a drink.

FIFTEEN

I SAUNTER CASUALLY UP THE sidewalk, Jase by my side. I am a squirming bundle of nerves inside at the prospect of Elliot chewing me out, but outwardly I attempt cool, calm, and collected.

"Here we are," I say at the door to Elliot's studio, handing Jase my helmet. "Meet me back here in a few hours?"

Jase looks uncomfortable and scans the sidewalk on both sides of us.

"What?" I ask him.

Jase breathes out audibly. "If you run, my father will fucking kill me. Literally."

"Wait, you think I'm going to run?"

Jase shrugs. "I would if I were you."

I point to a Hooters across the road. "You can keep an eye on me *and* order beer from hot girls with nice racks," I say. "What do you say?"

He shifts from foot to foot. "I'll just come in with you," he says.

"Wait," I say, putting my palm flat against his chest. "If you must know, I kind of … cried last time I got tattooed. And he told me the coloring in is worse than the outline."

Jase relaxes perceptibly and steps back. "Okay," he says. "Well, I'll be just across the road."

I smile sweetly. "Thanks."

I wait patiently until he has crossed the road, wave him off and take a deep breath, pushing the heavy glass door to Elliot's studio open. The bell above the door chimes to signal that someone has entered, and I jump ten feet in the air.

Elliot is tattooing a butterfly on some woman's lower back when I walk in. He notices me immediately and stops his work, the gun clattering onto the tray beside him.

"Okay," he says to her. "We're all done for today. Make sure to give us a call next week and book in for your final appointment."

The lady sits up, a look of confusion on her face. "Aren't you gonna finish it now?" she asks.

Elliot squirts her skin with a layer of antiseptic solution and tapes a piece of plastic-backed gauze on top. "Nope," he says. "You're bleeding too much. Have you been drinking, ma'am?"

The guilty look on her face provides an answer. Elliot gently but firmly pushes her out of the door, promising that her finished tatt will look just gorgeous next week. Once she leaves, he spins around to face me.

"Where the *hell* have you been?" he asks, his expression frustrated.

I smile in case Jase can see us from here. "We're being watched," I say to him through my cotton-candy grin. "Are you gonna take me back there and color me in, or what?"

His entire demeanor changes when he understands that there are eyes on us, and he points to the table that the old lady had been prostrate on only moments before.

I take my shirt off and hang it over the seat beside the table, my breasts covered by a plain black bra that is struggling to contain their ample size. Elliot seems a little flustered, and I grin wickedly. "You like them?" I ask him, waiting for him to bite. "I got them for a good price."

"Shut up and get on the table, whatever your name is," he says, and I can't tell if he is amused or annoyed.

I hoist myself onto the table and lay down, wincing as I rip my bandage off in one go. "They're just boobs, El," I say, settling against the squeaky plastic.

He takes a moment to look at them dubiously before shifting his attention to my face. "They're hot. I don't want to talk about your boobs, though." He snaps a plastic bag open and withdraws a single-use needle chock full of ink that will stain my skin permanently.

"I want to talk about where the fuck you've been for three days not answering my calls." His words are bitter and I can tell he has thought of nothing else except me and my safety since I left here three days ago.

"I'm sorry," I say quietly. "They took my phone and smashed it."

"Well, are you okay?" he asks me, his voice straining to sound normal under the weight of his despair. His blue eyes are oceans of worry and hurt, and I have to look away before I really do cry.

"I'm fine," I say. "I got in there. They bought my story. That's it."

"That's it?" Elliot stops fumbling with needles and packages and stares at me questioningly. "What do you mean, that's it?"

I grit my teeth and take a deep breath, the events of the past three days a broken record of pain, blood, and lust playing on repeat in my addled mind. I can't tell him about Michael. He would never speak to me again if he knew the depths of my treachery.

"Dornan liked me straightaway," I say in a monotone voice. "He liked me a little too much."

Elliot's hands are empty and I can hear his nails digging into the hard plastic that covers the table I lay upon. "Julz…" he growls.

Hot tears fill my eyes and I look up at him angrily. "Don't call me that," I say viciously. "Don't you ever call me that, do you understand? Do you want us to both get killed?"

He lets go of the table and shakes his head. "Did he hurt you?" he asks, his fists in tight balls.

"Yes," I say honestly, blinking the tears away. "But I let him. It's all part of the act."

He goes to grab my shoulders and I look at the front door in alarm. "Jason is watching," I say in a high-pitched voice, and I see Elliot use every single reserve of strength he has to back away from me and collect his tattoo gun from the counter. He preps the needles, each one holding dye that will soon be on my skin.

"How'd you convince him to stay out there, anyway?" Elliot is crazy angry, but attempting normal conversation at the same time. *Super.*

I stretch out on the soft plastic bed. "I told him I cried last time I got inked, and it would be way too embarrassing for me if he watched."

Elliot smirks despite his earlier tirade, his needle poised at my hipbone.

"So," he asks stonily, "you gonna cry?"

I clench my fists as he begins to drag sharp needles through the sensitive, scarred flesh that covers my hipbone. "Hell, no. It takes more than a little tattoo gun to make this girl cry."

SIXTEEN

THREE HOURS LATER, MY TATTOO is completely shaded in, blacks and dark reds a swirl of patterns and seeping blood across my midsection. I am sweating, and my skin is simultaneously numb and screaming alight, each nerve crying its own confused protest.

"I thought this wasn't supposed to hurt," I asked Elliot as he applied a new dressing. "I thought I was meant to get a huge rush or something?"

Elliot paused, staring at the fresh blue and purple bruises around my wrists, where Dornan pinned me to the bed after he shot Michael.

"Your body only has so much adrenalin," he says, taking my wrist and studying the flesh with an unreadable look on his face. He brushes his warm fingertips lightly across the bruises, a deep frown settling into his forehead. "You've probably used it all up."

The front door jangles, scaring the hell out of me, and I look up to see Jase at the front counter of the shop. He eyes us cautiously, obviously noticing the tenderness with which Elliot is touching my bruised wrists.

"You done?" he asks me. I nod eagerly, sliding off the bench and carefully pulling my t-shirt back over my head. I wince as the fabric touches my inked skin; even though the plastic forms a barrier, it doesn't stop my skin from protesting at the merest touch.

"Don't forget to bathe it every day and keep it clean and dry," Elliot says, as he's no doubt said a thousand times before. He hands me an after-care kit which includes gauze pads, saline solution, barrier cream, and a business card with the landline of the studio printed across the front in large numbers. *Smart.*

"Got it!" I say, making my way towards the door, where Jase waits. I don't look back at Elliot. If I look back, I'm screwed.

Remember why you're here.

My mantra, a chant that keeps me sane in times of trepidation.

Fuck Dornan over. Kill his sons. Send the rest to jail. *Find that tape.*

Live happily ever after. *Pfft.*

We step outside to a day that has almost entirely disappeared; wisps of aubergine cloud hang low in the sky, waiting for the night sky to swallow them completely.

"Where to?" Jase asks, lowering his sunglasses to look at me.

I shrug. "I don't know. I'm kind of starving. Are you hungry?"

Jase smiles. "Yeah. I called the clubhouse, Pop's still sleeping it off."

He must notice my face fall as he says it, and back-pedals furiously. "I'm sorry," he stutters, "I didn't mean–"

"Beer," I say to him in response. "I could really use a beer."

He frowns and points to my midsection. "Are you sure you're supposed to drink after getting a tattoo done? Doesn't it bleed a lot or something?"

I shrug. "Let's find out."

He laughs, and the sound is sweet in a world full of hurt and lies. "Come on, then," he says. "I know a place on the beach that you'll probably like. You eat Mexican food?"

I think of how, as teenagers, we would visit Venice Beach to get away from our parents, where we would drink cheap beer and order nachos after swimming in the sea for hours upon hours. I swallow a lump in my throat and smile. "Sounds great," I say.

As we make our way towards the beach, only a couple hundred meters away, I can't get the past three hours out of my head. The conversation with Elliot was a roller coaster, to say the least.

"What's your game plan, anyway?" Elliot spoke carefully as he pressed sharp needles into my flesh.

I was already bathed in sweat, my fingers curled around the sides of the bed. "I'm going to take them out, one by one. Dornan last." I breathed heavily to the hum of the gun.

"Take them out?" Elliot had muttered. "What do you mean, exactly?"

I locked eyes with him and he stepped away from me, his gun poised in his hand, silenced for the moment.

"You mean to tell me you're going to kill all of them?"

I smiled darkly, and I could tell he was grasping for a way to talk me out of it.

"You should have stayed in Nebraska," he said through gritted teeth. "This is insane."

"Why?" I challenged him. "Because they don't deserve to die?"

The tattoo gun dropped to his side and he looked frustrated. "Because it shouldn't have to be you who does it," he said with an air of finality.

"Elliot?" I asked. "Hey." I sat up and reached across the void that separated us, touching the intricate ink sleeve that adorned his muscled arm.

"I'm sorry I couldn't do it for you," he said, looking completely defeated. "I wanted to. I didn't think about anything else. And then ..."

"I understand," I said, feeling robbed that I couldn't pull him to my chest and give him the biggest, tightest hug. Instead, I focused on his arm, and the tattoos that adorned it. There were stars and skulls, a pretty pin-up girl with blonde hair, a babushka doll, a sickle, and a gun. Birds were scattered in the spaces not

taken by other symbols, and I swallowed thickly as I realized I was staring at the story of his life without me. I brushed my fingertip lightly against the babushka doll, certain it was for his daughter.

"You have something to live for, El. Something far more important than revenge. You have a family."

He smiled sadly and looked down at where my fingers lay on his skin.

"Kayla was an accident," he said, rubbing his finger across the babushka doll. He raised his t-shirt sleeve and I saw the word Kayla captured in a swirling red ribbon across his shoulder. "Mandy wanted to have a termination, but–"

My breathing stilled for a moment at that word.

"I wouldn't let her," he murmured. "I told her what it was really like to watch that happen. God, I'm sorry, Julz," he finished, and I didn't bother correcting him. "I didn't mean to mention that shit."

I smiled through my sadness. "Don't be sorry," I replied, my heart swelling and twisting for Elliot with an emotion I hadn't felt in years. "I'm happy something so nice came out of something so horrible."

He relaxed and held up his tattoo gun again. "We should finish this."

I nodded and lay back down. "Yeah."

He poised the needle above my skin. "Which one first?" he asked, and I immediately knew what he was asking. Which one was I going to kill first.

"Chad," I replied softly. "The oldest one." The worst one.

He nodded and I tensed as he gouged sharply into my flesh.

SEVENTEEN

"HEY. EARTH TO SAMANTHA!" JASE is waving a hand in front of my face. We have stopped at the end of the Venice Beach boardwalk and all of the crazy that lies along it. I can see a guy juggling fire, a middle-aged Filipino woman belting out bad karaoke, and plenty of body builders still working out at the bank of metal gym equipment that sits in the sand.

Memories of being a teenager flood through me. It even *smells* the same. I have to force myself to pay attention to Jase as he speaks.

"You want to eat?" he asks me.

I shake my head. "Let's swim," I say, drawn to the ocean like a magnet. I kick my borrowed shoes off and leave them on the sidewalk, stepping off into the gloriously warm sand. It feels blissful. It feels like home.

Jase smirks. "We don't have bathing suits."

I shrug. "My underwear will work," I say, tugging my shirt off and throwing it on the ground beside the shoes. I unzip my pants and shimmy them down, kicking them onto the pile as well. I am wearing only a black bra and matching bikini-cut panties, and I know I look good.

I look back at Jase and laugh. "Come on," I say. "Unless you're scared."

"Scared of getting arrested," he says devilishly. "I don't wear underwear."

"Oh," I say, raising an eyebrow. "Well, at least roll those jeans up and step into the water with me."

I leave him on the sidewalk, cussing at his laced boots as he tries to pull them off, and run across the sand and into the water. Diving underneath the surface, I keep my eyes firmly closed in case my contact lenses should become dislodged. Between my tattoo, my contact lenses, and trying to remember my fake name, keeping this disguise up is starting to get really annoying. *And it's only the beginning.*

I surface again and kick my legs, the salt water a welcome cleansing from the horrors of the past few days.

Jase hovers at the edge of the water. His toes are barely getting wet. He has removed his leather jacket and shirt, and I can appreciate his six-pack and build from where I float lazily. The gangly boy I left has morphed into a very attractive man. His tattoos are completely different to Elliot's – mostly gang related – and when he turns to look up the beach, I catch sight of his Gypsy Brothers tattoo. It looks identical to the one Dornan sports, and my stomach roils. *Turn around, Jase.*

He does, wading in a little deeper so that the water laps at his ankles. "Come out here, you pussy," I tease him.

"My jeans'll get wet," he says. I stick my lip out and pout dramatically. He laughs at that.

"The water's soooo good," I say. He fishes his keys and cell phone out of his pocket, throwing them on the sand just out of the water's reach. Nobody will touch them. He's a Gypsy Brother. They pretty much own Venice Beach.

He strides into the water, up to his knees. The bottom of his jeans are immediately soaked with salt water.

"Further," I call, kicking backwards.

He shakes his head and doesn't move. I swim towards him, a devilish grin on my face. "Don't–" he warns, but before he can finish his sentence, I pull his arms, making him keel over into the water. He surfaces, laughing and spluttering, and my heart feels a little less heavy.

"Thanks," he says, his voice dripping with sarcasm.

"Welcome," I reply. "Told you the water was good."

He just shakes his head, smiling in amusement.

He watches the horizon for a moment before speaking more seriously. "So are you, like, my dad's old lady now?"

I almost choke. "What?" I splutter.

"My pop. Are you guys, like, an item?"

My smile is completely gone, and I press my feet firmly to the sand beneath us. But he has posed an interesting question. Does Dornan consider us in a relationship, no matter how short our acquaintance has been, no matter how blatantly dysfunctional?

"I don't know," I say honestly. Because I don't. The unexpected closeness with Dornan has presented both a blessing and a curse – I have unparalleled access to him, his club, and his sons, but at the same time, if I continue, I will have to spend the majority of my time with the person I hate more than anything in the entire world, the person who ripped my entire existence apart and stole everything I ever cared about.

"I think he's pretty smitten," Jase says, and I don't know what I hear in his voice – jealousy? Resignation?

I shrug. "I only just met the man. All I wanted was a job at your burlesque club."

I didn't want him to shoot my supposed ex-boyfriend – an innocent stranger – and then hold a gun to my head.

"My father's not the kind of person you say no to," he says seriously, squinting into the sun.

"And here we are," I reply.

He doesn't talk for a few moments, and I use the time to swim in a slow circle around him.

"I'm sorry about my brother, hopped up on fucking energy drinks," he says finally.

"Pardon?" I ask, stopping my breaststroke. I float in front of him, then put my feet back onto firm sand.

"Chad," he says, chewing his lip thoughtfully. "People always think he's high, but he's not. He drinks those goddamn guarana drinks from the minute he gets up in the morning. Guy's gonna have a heart attack one of these days. I've tried telling him, but ..."

I can only imagine how that conversation went.

"I like those drinks," I say, laughing. "Almost as much as I like beer."

"Don't touch the ones in the fridge back at the clubhouse," he says. "Chad'll murder you in your sleep. They're all his apparently."

I smile vacantly, a twisted idea beginning to form in my mind.

Guy's gonna have a heart attack one of these days.

My smile turns into a shit-eating grin.

"What?" Jase asks, flicking water in my face.

"Nothing," I say, flicking water back. "I was just thinking about how good that beer would be right now."

We drag dry clothes onto our wet bodies, and they cling to our skin as we drink beer and eat fish tacos on the sidewalk. It grows dark and I watch the fire juggler absently, thinking over the details of my plan.

My mind is suddenly racing so fast that I can barely concentrate on what Jase is saying.

Because I think I have figured out how I am going to kill Chad.

And it will be delicious.

EIGHTEEN

IT TAKES A WEEK TO organize my little plan, all the while being fucked by Dornan at every opportunity he can find. He fucks me in the shower, in his office, in his bed, and over a pool table. I thank the stars that he has not thought to fuck me on the stage of the burlesque club, because if he did, I think I would evaporate under the burden of my lies and he would surely guess that my real name is Juliette Portland.

Ten days after my arrival, I enact my plan. It is a quiet Sunday afternoon in the clubhouse, and Chad is alone in the massive garage where all of the bikes are parked. There aren't many bikes here today – Dornan and most of the club have gone on a ride, and Chad has had to stay back, having just had his knee operated on. I can immediately tell that he is pissed off at being left, and he is hobbling around furiously, clanging spanners and swearing at his bike as it sits on its stand, most of its parts on the floor in messy piles.

I saunter in and close the door behind me, an open can of his favorite energy drink in my hand.

"Hey, Chad," I say, tilting the can as if I am drinking it. I don't let a drop of the liquid touch my lips, though.

I mean, *I* don't want to die.

Chad looks up, wearing an annoyed look, and his eyebrows bank together when he sees me.

"What the fuck do you want?" he asks, clanging more tools around. He does a double-take and stands up again, hobbling around the bike to me. He snatches the can out of my hand and I feign surprise. "Don't drink my fucking drinks, bitch," he says, slamming the can onto the counter next to him. I wait patiently as he continues to work on the bike.

"I didn't think you'd mind," I say, leaning on the counter next to him, making sure he has a good view of my cleavage. It's always a great distraction. "You shouldn't drink so much of that stuff, you know. Your body can't handle it."

He snorts and throws his spanner to the ground, narrowly missing the bike. He reaches for the can and takes a giant gulp, sneering at me. Bingo.

"What the fuck you smiling at, bitch?" he asks, slamming the can back down beside me. Almost immediately, he appears confused, and I can only imagine how fast his heart is starting to beat. He becomes drenched in sweat instantly, and sways on his feet.

I shrug, making my eyes wide and innocent. "Feeling okay, Chad?" I ask, laughing as he crashes to his knees. He screams as his freshly reconstructed knee makes a meaty pop and a cracking noise, and I can only guess that the operation has been reversed quite severely.

"What the–?" he pants, clutching his chest with both his hands. I kneel in front of him so that we are eye to eye, and pat his head condescendingly.

"There, there," I mock him as if he were a dog, "it'll all be over soon, *Chad.* You won't suffer as long as you made me suffer. That's unfortunate, but necessary."

His eyes blank out for a second, and I shuffle backwards, not wanting to be pinned by his burly weight when he keels over in about ten seconds.

"Who are you?" he splutters, holding his chest.

I smile as a feeling of supreme triumph washes over me. I kneel in front of him and lean close to his ear, my breath on his skin the last thing he will ever feel. "My name is Juliette," I whisper, "and you just got fucked, Chad."

I climb to my feet and continue to watch as he struggles.

"You bitch," he spits, his face turning red. He keels over, his shoulder hitting the floor with a solid *thwack*.

It takes forever for him to die.

When he is good and dead, I smile. Because it feels good. It feels even better than I thought it would.

One motherfucker down. Six to go. I wipe my fingerprints off the can, place it back on the bench, and step over Chad's motionless body. Making my way out of the garage with the tenacity of a stealthy cat, I head to the roof unseen. Along the way, I grab a beer from the fridge and knock the lid against the timber bench to pry it loose. Taking the stairs quickly and quietly, I burst onto the roof. Jase is sitting in a beanbag he has dug up from somewhere, watching the sun set over Venice Beach. I stand behind him, admiring the view.

"Hey," he says. "I just came out to watch the sunset before I go to work."

I sit cross-legged on the enormous beanbag beside him, sinking into the beans, my body so tired, so spent.

"You even brought me a beer," he jokes, gesturing to my full Corona. I smile and take a sip, holding it in front of him. "Here," I say. "I only wanted a taste."

His hand brushes mine as he takes the bottle from me, and I wait a second too long before I let go. Our eyes lock together, a dark worry settling over his features as he, too, must feel the spark that alights between us.

"Samantha–" he says.

I shake my head. "Don't."

He frowns and takes a swig of beer. "Don't what?"

I stare at my hands. "Don't say it."

He takes a long, deep breath and lets it out in a whoosh. "How do you know what I was going to say?"

I put my hand back over his, both of us gripping the bottle. "I just do," I reply, squeezing his hand tight.

I think about how much I love him, how much I have always loved him, and it is enough to make me sob. But I don't. I can't.

I'm not finished yet.

There are still so many things I have to do.

I HAVE LIED.

I have cheated.

I have given my body and my life to the man who destroyed my family and left me for dead.

I have killed, I have sinned, and worst of all, I have enjoyed the misery of others.

I have licked the salty tears of a father mourning his firstborn son, and nothing has ever tasted so sweet.

I have died, and I have been resurrected, a phoenix from the ashes.

I know I'm going to hell. I'll burn in the fiery pits alongside Dornan and his sons for the things I've done, and for the things I'm about to do.

But I don't care. It will be worth every lick of the devils flames on my guilty flesh to destroy Dornan Ross.

One motherfucker down. Six to go.

SIX BROTHERS, THE FOLLOW-UP TO *SEVEN SONS*, WILL BE
RELEASED IN FEBRUARY 2014.

TO STAY UP TO DATE WITH RELEASES, VISIT
LILISTGERMAIN.BLOGSPOT.COM

KEEP READING FOR AN EXCLUSIVE LOOK AT THE FIRST CHAPTER
OF *SIX BROTHERS* (GYPSY BROTHERS, #2) BY LILI SAINT
GERMAIN…

———

"To be wronged is nothing, unless you continue to remember it."
- Confucius

I would never forget. And so, for me, being wronged was everything.

———

SOME PEOPLE WOULD CALL ME a whore. A girl who sold her soul to the devil. Who let him inside her, with no remorse. Who danced with the monster who destroyed everything.

To those people, I say only this: I didn't have to sell Dornan Ross my soul. He already owned it. And once I've killed him, maybe I can get it back.

When I think about life before Juliette Portland supposedly died, I think of the midday sun, and the way it caught the water, making a million tiny diamonds glisten in the Venice Beach waves. I think of laughter and first kisses, of ice-cream and stolen beer and ferris wheels.

I think of how much I loved Jason Ross, and how valiantly he fought to protect me when the rest of his family were beating and fucking me to within an inch of my life.

I think about my father, and how whenever he was near, I felt safe, no matter what.

I think about my mother, and how indifferent she was to my existence, to the point where my father was going to take me away from everything, including her, so that we could have a life free of the constant danger that a club like the Gypsy Brothers meant.

I think of how, if he had succeeded, what a wonderful life that would have been.

It's true what they say - keep your friends close and your enemies closer. Only, they forgot to add: Don't keep your enemies so close that they can strike without warning. That was my father's mistake. That was our fatal undoing.

When I was planning my revenge, I vowed not to make the same mistakes he did. Allowing the enemy too close - Dornan was VP of the club, my father the President, but he was quickly losing control as Dornan and his sons outnumbered him.

I remember my final moments, before I blacked out, when Chad and Maxi were loading me into the back of a van to get me to the hospital.

"Why don't we just finish her and be done with it?" Chad asked his father as he struggled with my nearly-dead weight.

Dornan smacked the back of his eldest son's head and pointed to me, beaten, covered in blood, one of my eyes swollen shut and the other cracked open enough to see where they were taking me.

"We can't fucking kill her," Dornan spat. "She knows where the money is."

"What money?" Maxi echoed.

Dornan sighed. "Don't you boys fucking listen? The mil her daddy embezzled from this club while I was busy with you boys and your fucking mothers these past years."

Chad whistled, dropping me into the back of a van like a sack of soggy potatoes. "That's a lot of money."

I whimpered as my head connected with a hard floor.

"It is, son," Dornan agreed. "But it's not about the amount. It's about the principle, you understand?"

Chad nodded. "You don't steal from your own club."

"That's right. Now get this bitch to the hospital so we can find out what the fuck they did with my money."

"And then?"

I shivered, watching them from my spot on the dirty floor of the van.

Dornan sighed. "And then we finish her."

I vowed not to make the same mistakes my father did. But here, now, laying pinned beneath Dornan as he pummels me with his rage and grief, his eldest son dead by my hand and the funeral in just a few hours, I have to wonder if I'm heading down the exact path that led to our destruction all those years ago.

SIX BROTHERS WILL BE RELEASED ON FEBRUARY 16TH, 2014.

About the Author

Lili writes dark romance. Her debut serial novel, Seven Sons, was released in early 2014, with the following books in the series to be released in quick succession. Lili quit corporate life to focus on writing and is loving every minute of it. Her other loves in life include her gorgeous husband, good coffee, hanging at the beach and running. She loves to read almost as much as she loves to write

Word-of-mouth is crucial for any author to succeed. If you enjoyed the book, please consider leaving a review. Even if it's only a sentence of two, it makes a huge difference and would be very much appreciated.

Say Hello!

Lili always loves hearing from readers. You can find her in the following places:

www.lilistgermain.blogspot.com
lilisaintgermain@gmail.com

Made in the USA
Coppell, TX
23 April 2021